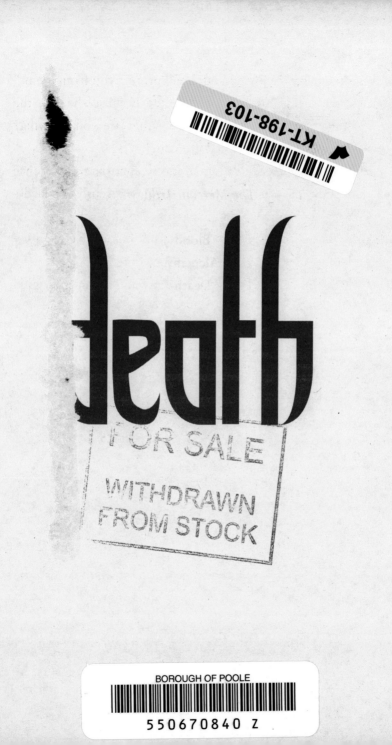

death

The Mercian Trilogy

Blood
Alchemy
Death

K J WIGNALL

death

First published in Great Britain in 2013
by Electric Monkey, an imprint of Egmont UK Limited
The Yellow Building, 1 Nicholas Road, London W11 4AN

Text copyright © 2013 K J Wignall

The moral rights of the author have been asserted

ISBN 978 1 4052 5862 3

1 3 5 7 9 10 8 6 4 2

www.electricmonkeybooks.co.uk

A CIP catalogue record for this title is available from the British Library

Typeset by Avon DataSet Ltd, Bidford on Avon, Warwickshire

Printed and bound in Great Britain by the CPI Group

48093/1

EGMONT

Our story began over a century ago, when seventeen-year-old Egmont Harald Petersen found a coin in the street. He was on his way to buy a flyswatter, a small hand-operated printing machine that he then set up in his tiny apartment.

The coin brought him such good luck that today Egmont has offices in over 30 countries around the world. And that lucky coin is still kept at the company's head offices in Denmark.

For L

1

Undead? Not I. It's true that I died, but to use the term undead does little to sum up my unique condition. Surely it's not enough to say what I am not, because the really important thing is what I am.

And what I am is death itself. I am pestilence and plague, war and turmoil. I am what you fear when the night is dark, I am the shiver you feel in your spine when you least expect it. I am the dreams from which you awake full of dread. I am the dreams from which one day you fear you will never wake at all.

How can I make so bold a claim? Because I alone was given the sight to see all that has happened, all that is, all that will be. After living for so long in ignorance, this knowledge has been my reward: the knowledge of past and future and my role within it.

It is a tale which has been told in many forms, the characters shifting, given different names, different parts to play. But all those tales come from the same source. All the monsters are only the Grykken in other forms.

All the heroes are the four kings of old who came to destroy the Grykken and claim its supernatural treasure.

This is the tale I will tell, told as if I have played no part in it and have no part to play. It is the tale of the Grykken. It is the tale of Sivard, and Archelaos, and Xiang Xi, and yes, it is the tale of Lorcan Labraid. It is the story of the Mercian Earls and all the others who ruled at Marland, the very history of Marland itself and the terrible things that happened there. And in being about all those things, it is also the story of William of Mercia and his destiny.

Yes, I will play the bard, imagining myself in a lit winter hall as of old, entertaining the warriors and their kinfolk with stories of bravery, taking their minds from the death that lurks in the darkened night. And as they listen and are swept away by legend, none will realise that it is death who speaks, that he is with them and among them, just as I stand at your shoulder now. I am death, and you will know me soon enough.

2

The snow was little more than a memory, and the dreams were getting worse. Since the battle at Wyndham's house and the loss of Marcus, they'd spent three weeks in Will's chambers under the cathedral. In her waking hours Eloise seemed to be coming to terms with what had happened, but he'd watched as her sleep had become gradually more troubled in that time.

If Wyndham's sorcery had so far failed to destroy Will, it had at least succeeded in unsettling Eloise. She spoke occasionally as she dreamt, and it was clear to Will that she was sometimes reliving that last conflict, picturing the wild and deranged vampires imprisoned in Wyndham's cellars, the fire with which Will and Eloise had destroyed the house, but above all the death of Marcus.

Once or twice she had even called out Marcus's name, as if trying to warn him of his impending fate. Will felt that keenly, and was still astonished that a boy brought to Marland to spy on them could so quickly

3

have become such a trusted ally and friend.

Eloise remembered those dreams, but there were others that she said she couldn't remember, or perhaps did not want to. At first Will had worried that it might be a return of the visions Wyndham had made her see in the labyrinth, but Eloise was convinced it wasn't. She was certainly comfortable around Will in her waking hours.

It still did not ease him as he sat watching her now, the anguish playing out across her sleeping face, the fretful mumbling. And as he sat there, he wished for one of his own waking visions, but they had completely ceased in the same period.

As much as he longed for his mind to drift, to find himself among those ruins with her, the sun warm on his skin, it would not come back to him. He wondered if it was because they were idling here, no longer moving forward, even though he knew the future he was moving towards could not offer him that sunlit afternoon anyway.

She turned, her eyes opening quite suddenly, and she saw him sitting there and smiled.

"Have I slept long?"

"Longer than ever – I think it's approaching midnight." That worried him too, the fact that she was seeing no daylight, that she'd hardly strayed into the outside world in three weeks, only a few visits to Rachel

4

and Chris after The Whole Earth had closed for the night. She needed sunlight and air and real living people.

She sat up. "It's strange – I don't feel I've slept long at all. Was I dreaming?"

He nodded and she smiled hopelessly and started to put on her boots. This had become their routine, and so Will stood and removed the stone that blocked the chamber door, then waited as Eloise finished tying her laces and picked up her smaller bag.

As she stood she said, "You know, you could have a guest bathroom installed down here – it would save all this trouble."

"But it's no trouble at all." And in truth, he enjoyed the routine of escorting her up to the cathedral toilets, waiting for her in the twilight of the nave, a ritual which had a deceptive air of permanence about it. "Besides, it won't be much longer. We should go back to Marland soon."

She'd just picked up the small torch she used to light her way, but hesitated. "It's too soon – I'm not ready."

Will feared she would never be ready if they stayed. The things she'd witnessed, the shock of losing Marcus, all seemed to be weighing on her mind more, not less, with each passing day. He had to give her a purpose, something else to concentrate on, even at the risk of sounding selfish.

"I understand that, but we know my destiny awaits me there, and only there. And the longer we wait, the stronger Wyndham will become again. He could be planning a new attack even now."

"I wonder if that's part of why I don't want to go back, not because of Wyndham, but the thought of your destiny – for some reason, I've started to worry about it not ending well for us." Will smiled, sympathetic, and was about to reply when Eloise said, "Can't we just stay here?"

"We can stay a little longer if you like, but there's something I want to show you in the cathedral."

His tone seemed to appease her and she set off into the tunnel. Will followed, once more enjoying the comforting aspects of the ritual – the tunnel and the steps, lifting the stone up into the crypt. All the things that had become mundane for him over the centuries had been given new meaning because he did them with her.

Even as he sat waiting for her in the back pew, looking along the nave of the church that had been his home for so many centuries, he could sympathise with her desire to stay, to avoid the very thing he'd so long hoped for. Because, in achieving it, he suspected the good things in his life would be swept away with the bad. Would he ever again have the simple pleasure of sitting here in the cathedral at night? Would he ever again know the completeness of spending time with Eloise?

With that thought, he heard her come back into the church and he stood to meet her. But seeing her face looking fresher, catching the scent of her toothpaste, only served to remind him that she was human, that this moment would pass whatever happened. If he spurned his fate now, he wouldn't be granting himself a few extra months or years with her, but an eternity without her.

As if hearing his thoughts, she said, "So, what did you want to show me?"

"My talisman." He reached out and took her hand, so warm in his, and led her along the side of the nave. He stopped near the organ loft and said, "Here it is. You'll need your torch."

She took her torch out of her bag and turned it on, aiming it carefully at the floor, as much to avoid the attention of people outside the cathedral as to protect Will's eyes.

"Where should I be aiming it?"

"Where you aim it now, at the floor."

Eloise looked down at the stone on which she was standing and said, "It's just a paving . . ." She stopped and got down on to her knees. "Oh my goodness, how beautiful. A fossil."

She traced her finger round the spiral of the ammonite, and Will could not help but remember that he had done the same as a small boy when his father had shown it to him, nearly eight hundred years earlier.

"Exposed quite by accident by the stonemasons, lodged here ever since. I was seven when my father first brought me to look at it."

She looked up. "Your father?" She seemed touched even by the mention of him.

Will nodded. "Yes, hard to believe, but I too was a child once. Yet some of those memories seem so vivid, so recent. I knelt exactly where you are now, traced the spiral of its shell just as you did."

"Did you know what it was back then?"

"The general belief was that fossils signified nothing, that they were nature's caprices. But some were more enlightened, my father among them. He wondered if this ammonite suggested there had once been an ocean covering this land. The ancient Greeks had already concluded as much, but in 1247 we were as far from them as we were from any future truth."

She'd been listening eagerly, all the while tracing the faint ridges with her fingertips, but now she lowered her eyes and stared at the fossil, and after a moment she said, "I know why you wanted me to see it, why you think of it as a talisman."

"Then you understand, Eloise, that I've been trapped too long already. And if I was trapped with you it would be a paradise, but in no time at all you too would be a fleeting memory."

She looked up at him, resigned, and said, "I know that." As she spoke, he heard another noise, high above, as if a bird had become trapped in the vault, but he'd heard it over her words and it had sounded bigger than a bird, much bigger. She didn't seem concerned, but said, "What's wrong?"

He put his finger to his lips and she immediately stood up. He could hear movement at ground level as well now, somewhere across the nave, perhaps in one of the side chapels. Eloise's eyes were darting about too.

She whispered, "There are people in here."

Will nodded because they weren't alone. But he took in the air and knew that there were no other people there, or at least nobody from among the living.

3

They looked about them. Suddenly a shadow flitted across the other side of the nave, partly obscured by the stone pillars that separated them. Even so, Eloise was quick to point her torch and the light flickered with the figure's swift movement.

Had it been a man? If so, he'd either been tall and powerful or it had been a trick of the light. And still Will could hear the noise high above. He looked up into the shadows, but was pulled away again by another disturbance at ground level.

Eloise said quietly, "Should we be nervous?" The fact that she was even able to ask the question said something of her character and of the things she'd already witnessed in the last few months.

Tiny amplified movements were sounding from several different directions, and Will quickly realised there were at least four of them. Not four people, but four *somethings*, and he was up here without a weapon of any sort.

He looked to the middle of the nave, between the pews and the choir stalls, at the large free-standing candlestick – it was taller than him and solid, cumbersome perhaps, but a formidable weapon in his hands. He gestured for Eloise to follow him and they quickly covered the short distance to the candlestick.

He couldn't see any of the creatures, even the one that could still be heard somewhere up in the vaulted roof, but he continued to pick up the sound of odd little movements, possibly footsteps. He looked along the aisle stretching out in front of them, the pews, the pillars either side.

Eloise was looking too and said, "Should I shine my torch anywhere?"

"No, I can see, but they're out of sight somewhere."

"What are they?"

Will slowly shook his head in response, even as he heard another noise further down the nave. And then, without further warning, the sound high above became a whoosh and a shadow dropped from the vault and landed halfway down the aisle. Its descent was swift and yet the creature landed with incredible grace and stood facing them as its leathery wings folded behind it.

What it was, Will couldn't be sure, except some form of demon. Its body was almost human, albeit tall and powerful, but it had bat-like wings and its face was that of a devil. In fact it looked exactly like the devils depicted in religious art across many centuries.

"Oh my God," said Eloise, astonished, even awestruck, rather than terrified. The devil turned at the sound of her voice and stared at her, its eyes glowing red in the half-light of the church. It sniffed the air, its upper lip drawing back in the process to reveal a row of jagged teeth. "It's like a gargoyle."

"Except rather bigger," said Will. He saw too that this gargoyle carried a sword which at the moment was hanging casually from its right hand. He was about to tell her what he planned to do, how he would use the candlestick as a weapon, when there was more movement further down the nave and the other three emerged and slowly walked up the aisle to join their companion.

They were all the same type of creature, but just as the stonemasons of Will's time would vary their gargoyles, giving them individual characteristics, so each of these creatures had a distinct appearance. One had pointed ears which stuck out; another had a mouth that seemed frozen in a permanent grimace. Even from this distance, Will could also see that their swords differed from each other in design, but each of them carried one.

The four of them stood in a line, looking at Will with some curiosity, their heads tilting this way and that as if trying to get a better look at him. Then, as one, they started walking slowly forward, at what seemed an almost ceremonial pace. The swords, for the moment, still hung by their sides.

Will said, "I'm going to use this candlestick, but I have no idea how powerful these creatures are, so be prepared."

"I don't suppose my torch will be much use on this occasion."

He looked at her and smiled, then reached out and put one hand on the cold metal column of the candlestick. But as he did so, the devils stopped their progress, and even with their demonic features it looked as if they were uncertain, perhaps wary of having done something wrong.

It was a strange sensation, but in that moment Will got the impression they were afraid of him. He lowered his hand again, wanting to reinforce any notion they might have that he had nothing to fear from them. They started to walk again, lowering their heads a little as they got closer, and when they were maybe ten paces short of where Will and Eloise stood, they came to a halt.

The one which had shown itself first dropped down on to one knee. Still with its head bowed, it took hold of the sword blade with its left hand and placed it on the floor, the hilt towards Will. The others immediately followed suit, dropping to their knees, laying down their swords, so that all four were arrayed with the hilts towards Will. For all the world, it appeared to be an act of supplication.

The first suddenly expanded its wings and catapulted into the air, swooping up into the vault. The other three followed, one at a time, as if to avoid getting their wings entangled, taking flight and arcing up in formation into the high vault before disappearing.

The noise quickly faded, suggesting they'd found their way out of the cathedral, and all that was left now was the faintest sulphurous odour, as of burned matches perhaps, and the remnants of fire. And the four swords.

Eloise looked down at them, took a step forward, then turned and looked at Will again as she said, "So the gargoyles are on our side?"

He smiled at the fact that even now she was in no doubt that it was "our side" rather than "your side". He was certain he'd seen creatures resembling these on the labyrinth walls at Marland, was equally certain that they had probably formed part of the visions Wyndham had forced upon Eloise, visions that had so very nearly turned her against Will. And yet now her faith in him seemed as unshakeable as ever.

"They meant us no harm, which is some relief in itself."

"Will, they were in awe of you, and this . . ." She

14

gestured to the swords on the floor. "That's an act of tribute if ever I saw one."

He walked forward, bent down and carefully picked up one of the swords. He'd expected some shock or sensation to hit him upon touching it, for his soul to find some resonance in these weapons, but there was nothing. It was just a sword.

"The four swords, the four vampire kings, their bloodlines meeting in my person. It was most certainly a tribute, though not one I would have chosen for myself."

Eloise knelt down, but seemed eager to avoid actually touching any of the swords. Still, she studied them carefully and said, "Do you think these are the actual swords? They're certainly different designs – it suggests they belonged to very different people."

Will looked at the blade of the weapon he held, pristine, unblemished by time. Those kings had first lived at least a thousand years ago, and probably much more than that, and these swords could not have survived in such a condition over all that time. Unless, of course, they had been protected by the same wickedness which also preserved Will and the others of the undead.

He dropped down to one knee so that he was facing her and said, "Whatever they are, something must have happened in the weeks that we've been here, some movement about the axis of my destiny. The time has come, Eloise, to act, whether we wish it or not."

She looked a little nervous, but said, "So you want to go back?"

Will nodded. "Tomorrow, but first I want to visit the library. It's something I've been meaning to do for weeks, but I thought you might not want to be reminded . . . of what happened to the Reverend Fairburn."

"You could have gone while I was asleep," she said.

"No, I couldn't." He didn't need to spell it out, that he would not have left her alone while she slept. Eloise smiled, touched.

He smiled too, and stood up, taking her by the hand and helping her back to her feet. "Besides, this is something we do together or not at all."

He put the sword back on the floor and she said, "Are you leaving the swords here?"

"Until we get back. I don't think we'll need them in the library, and I have every confidence they'll still be here when we return."

They walked back the way they'd come, passing over the ammonite without even noticing it now. And in the back of Will's mind, a part of him hoped the swords wouldn't be there when they got back, the part of him that, like Eloise, was not sure that it wanted to follow the path that was finally beginning to reveal itself.

4

He led her by the hand as they climbed the spiral staircase, and turned on the lights only when they reached the first part of the library, the narrow room that sat at the top of it, books lining each of the two long walls, tricking casual observers into thinking this was all there was to it.

They walked halfway along, and as with the last time they'd visited, Will said, "Left or right?"

"Well, as we went left before, how about right this time?"

He nodded, wondering if in some small way she was trying to banish the memory of finding Fairburn in there, of him falling to his death. At least as they stepped out into the library proper, the lights were not on, so they could be reasonably sure of being alone this time.

Will turned on the lights and started out across the small wooden bridge, then stopped as once again Eloise was captivated by the eccentric complexity all around and below them, the bridges at odd angles, balconies, exposed portions of staircases, all overladen with books.

"Escher," she said, almost to herself, a reminder of her original suggestion that it looked like an optical illusion. She turned to Will. "What is it you want to look at?"

"Henry's Doomsday Book. I realised I've never looked at the entry for Marland Abbey, and as Henry seemed to know so much about the place, it occurred to me some of it might be in the book."

"Do you want me to lead the way?"

He laughed and beckoned her on, through small chambers and across bridges, down into the depths and back up a little way until they reached the chamber with the Doomsday Book. He opened it on its vast stand and turned the pages to the point where Marland would be found.

Eloise leaned over the book too, scanning the pages as Will turned them, then saying, "No, stop, we've gone past it."

She was right. Will turned back a page or two, but realised then that Marland simply wasn't in there.

"Why would he not include Marland?"

Eloise shrugged. "You said he made this after the Dissolution – maybe he felt bad about the monastery, maybe it was sensitive because he'd taken the land."

Will shook his head, doubting that any earl of the time would have omitted a place for such petty reasons.

Then, as he looked at the two open pages on which Marland should have appeared, he realised that they didn't match. He pushed the book open further and there between the two mismatched pages was a sliver of vellum where another page had been cut out.

Eloise stared at it, immediately sensing its significance as she said, "You think Wyndham removed it? But surely if it contained something strange, you would have noticed it before – I mean, you've been coming in here for what, five hundred years?"

"Something like that. But I never suspected the importance of Marland before now. I might have looked through this book without realising it was missing, it's true, but I might also have flipped past the entry for Marland without a second thought."

"Good, so we don't know if this page was removed last week or five hundred years ago."

"No, we only know that it was removed for a reason." Will looked at her, his gaze a little apologetic because he knew how reluctant she was to return there.

She gave him a resigned smile in response and said, "You win, OK? But we're not going till tomorrow, right?"

"No. One more day in my chambers."

Eloise looked suddenly concerned, and reached out and touched his cheek as she said, "Don't say it like that."

"I didn't mean that we would never return here." He smiled reassurance, but actually he suspected he *had* meant that, because he couldn't help but wonder if he was seeing all of these things for the last time.

And with that thought, he wanted to tour the library, the cathedral, all the places with which he had become so familiar, committing them to memory or bidding them farewell. He wouldn't though, in part to assuage Eloise's suspicions, in part because he wanted to hold on to the possibility of being wrong.

They made their way back to the crypt, stopping in the nave to collect the four swords. And only when they got back to his chambers, and he had placed the swords on one of the chests, did Eloise say, "Will you take them with you?"

"I hadn't thought about it – I imagine they were given to me for a reason."

"Then you should take them."

He nodded and she sat down on the edge of the daybed, and even though they were soon to leave, he became aware again of how limited her life had been with him these past few weeks. Even over the months since November, she had given up too much to be with him.

"Would you like to go out somewhere? I suspect it's too late to visit Chris and Rachel, but we could walk if you wish, or . . ."

Eloise shook her head and started to unlace her boots. "If this is our last night here, even for a while, let's just stay and talk. Tell me about your childhood."

She pushed herself back on to the daybed and Will laughed and sat next to her, because he had told her of his childhood so often that she probably knew it better than he did. Yet she never tired of hearing about it, never ran out of new questions to ask.

They talked for hours, long after the telltale prickling on his skin that heralded the dawn, and it was perhaps mid-morning before she fell asleep. He moved away from the daybed then and sat on his chair and waited for her dreams to show themselves.

He didn't need to wait long. Within an hour she started to mumble, her face forming into spasms of stress and alarm. Gradually it eased and she was at peace for a while before the pattern repeated itself. During the second period he could hear indistinct noises somewhere beyond his chambers.

He stood next to the stone blocking the entrance and listened. Perhaps his ears had deceived him because he could hear nothing now. Even so, he wanted to check, but wouldn't move the stone, not while she was sleeping.

She turned and mumbled, "You can't." She said something else then, something unintelligible. A chill ran along Will's spine and, unaccountably, he became aware of a presence somewhere close by, not outside his chambers now, but inside.

He looked around the room, uneasy. Eloise turned again and faced the wall. Will glanced at the swords, but decided against taking one, knowing full well that nothing solid had entered these rooms. He looked through into the chamber where his casket lay buried, then walked into the chamber with the pool. Both were empty.

He went back into the main room and stopped abruptly. Obscuring Eloise and the daybed from view, seven robed figures stood with their backs to him. Even after all this time, he tensed for a moment before realising that these were allies, not enemies, the seven witches who stood as if staring down at the sickbed of someone beloved.

None of them turned, but he heard the familiar voice say, "She dreams of you, William of Mercia."

"The things Wyndham made her see?" It was an abiding fear that Eloise still mistrusted him, still subconsciously believed the visions Wyndham had implanted within her.

"No. She dreams of the truth, of all the possible truths." The witch turned now, even as the others continued their bedside vigil, but her head remained bowed, her face obscured, as she said, "Your time is at hand, Wyndham's too, and Lorcan Labraid's. All that has been said now must be done."

"That's all very well, but I still know nothing of what it is that awaits me, or what I must do."

"You will." She looked up, and even with the shadowy absence of her face, he could tell that she was staring at him, fixing him with a gaze across nearly eight centuries. "Know this too, William of Mercia. I cursed your family once before, but if you allow any harm to befall this girl, I will bring a curse of a different order upon you and all of yours."

"I won't. You must know that I won't."

"I know that you wish not to. That is not the same."

She lowered her head again, signalling it seemed that the conversation was at an end.

"Will we see you again?"

"Only once, if you do not fail. It is in your hands alone now."

She began to turn, but Will said, "Wait, one more thing." She stopped. "Who is Eloise? Why . . .?"

She raised her head again, reducing him to silence. She appeared to think about the question for a moment, then said, "She is the reason we are here, but you knew that, you have always known that, and always will."

Another question formed, but no sooner had the last word emerged from her than the seven robes collapsed

23

into the floor and disappeared. Eloise was brought back into view, sleeping peacefully now, and even as those questions continued to rage round Will's head, he moved closer and sat in his chair, renewing his own vigil.

What new dangers did she face? Given what they had already experienced these last months, what did the witches believe might lie ahead that they doubted Will again, doubted him even to the point of threatening curses on him and his family?

The only reassurance Will could take was that the witch did not seem to doubt his ability to keep Eloise safe, only his determination. And if she had been able to see inside his heart, she would not have doubted even that.

He had intended to wake Eloise at ten, but she was dreaming and he feared waking her then, lest she be left with memories of what had been troubling her sleeping mind. Instead he waited for her to settle again, then placed his hand on her arm and gently called her name.

He could see her slowly returning from the depths in response to his voice, a long journey back to consciousness, and it touched him that she smiled before finally finding her way back and waking up. He smiled down at her and said, "We need to go soon, if we're to get to The Whole Earth just after closing."

Eloise nodded, then looked puzzled. "You want Chris and Rachel to take us? I would've thought you'd prefer a taxi."

"I've given that some thought. Your return to the school can't be kept secret, so Wyndham will know we're there. But if Chris is working for Wyndham, as I think we both now suspect, then I might learn something from the way he responds to our request."

"OK. Let me get my stuff together." She sat up, looking around the chamber, then stood. And as she got her bags together, he took a blanket and wrapped the four swords in it.

Once they were ready, Eloise turned on her torch, pointing it at the floor, and the two of them moved around the room blowing out the candles. Will lifted the stone from the entrance, but was immediately dazzled by something reflecting the torchlight. At the same time he heard the tinkling sound of falling metal.

He put the stone down quickly and looked at his feet, which were completely covered by a carpet of gold coins and jewels that had spilled into his chamber. The floor of the passageway beyond was almost knee-deep with them, the glare dazzling even without the torchlight upon them.

"Oh my God!" Eloise bent down and picked up a handful of coins and jewels, studying them in the torchlight. "Where? I mean . . . How? Did you know, did you hear? I mean . . ."

"I thought I heard noises last night, but then the witches came, so I connected the noises with them."

"So maybe it was them that did this." She stopped and looked up at him. "Hold on, the witches came?"

He nodded. "They were watching you as you dreamt. She told me we would only see them once more, and . . ."

"And?"

"She said the time was at hand, and that if I allowed anything to happen to you, I would be cursed." He laughed. "It's hard to believe I could be any more cursed than I am already, but I believed her all the same."

Eloise looked full of questions, but in the end she let the treasure fall from her fingers and settled for asking, "But you don't think they left all this?" Before he could respond, she answered her own question. "It doesn't seem like their style somehow."

Will shook his head and didn't bother to spell out who might be responsible. It was another tribute, that much was clear, probably from the very devils they'd encountered in the church, or by others like them. It was a tribute to him too, whereas the witches had always made it quite clear that their service was to Eloise.

He didn't bother to close the stone back over the

chamber entrance, and wasn't even sure how he could without first clearing away the treasure. That would have been an undertaking in itself, for they walked on that deep carpet of gold and gems all the way to the bottom of the steps that led up to the crypt.

Once or twice, Eloise stopped and crouched down to inspect some jewelled headband or brooch or coin. Will looked at them too, the coins bearing the faces of ancient kings and emperors from across the globe, all of them looking freshly minted, as if they had existed outside of time for a millennium or more.

"Keep some of them if you like."

She smiled. "I'm sure they'll still be here when we get back."

He shrugged, but then her face grew serious and he said, "What is it?"

"I just thought of something Elfleda said to you, and the kind of tribute this is." She waved her hand at the treasure, the torch beam rippling and glinting across it. "You're a king now, Will. They're treating you as a king."

He shook his head. "Not quite. And history is full of those who were nearly king, but never wore the crown. I fear we still have a way to go, and we won't know how far until we return to Marland."

Eloise nodded and walked on, reaching the bottom

of the steps. But even as they climbed to the crypt, her comment continued to trouble him. He was not yet a king, it was true, but that was clearly what they imagined for him. And what kind of kingship could he expect, what kind of kingdom, crowned by devils in a succession of evil?

5

The Whole Earth had just closed for the night, but Chris and Rachel were visible in the lit interior of the café, tidying the place at the end of the evening. Eloise knocked on the door and Rachel looked up to explain that they were closed before she saw who it was and smiled warmly.

She opened the door. "I was wondering why we hadn't seen you two for a few days." She noticed Eloise's bags and added, "Is this a good sign? Are you going back to school?"

"Will persuaded me it was time. We were hoping you might be able to take us back, unless you're busy. We can take a taxi . . ."

"Don't be silly, of course we'll take you."

Chris approached now, looking concerned beneath a casual veneer as he said, "Surely we won't be able to take you right up to the school at this time of night though. Or is it the new house you want us to take you to?"

Will looked at him. "It seems no one in the school is much concerned by Eloise's movements nowadays, so there would be nothing to stop us driving right to the door, but leaving us at the gate will be fine."

"Of course," said Chris with a nervous laugh. They'd only seen him a few times during these three weeks and yet he'd seemed increasingly troubled in some way. Or rather, he had been like a man trying to hide some terrible secret, the pressure of concealment building up inside him.

Rachel said, "Got time for a tea before you go?"

Eloise looked at her watch. "Well . . ."

"I'll put the kettle on," said Chris and walked into the house without waiting for confirmation.

Rachel raised her eyebrows, trying to make light of Chris's edgy behaviour, but once he was out of the room, Will said, "He seems troubled in some way."

She nodded, her concern rising to the surface. "He's been having nightmares for the last week or two, and I think it's affecting him. You can see he's a bit jumpy."

"How awful. I know how that feels," said Eloise.

Rachel said, "Yes, but you saw some terrible things at Wyndham's house, and your friend was killed, so yours are a little easier to explain."

"Perhaps Chris saw some terrible things too." They both looked at Will and he added by way of explanation, "If the nightmares have started quite suddenly and persisted for some time, perhaps something caused them."

Rachel looked to the door into the house, checking Chris wasn't coming back. Will could actually hear him, busy in the kitchen. Satisfied, she said, "He used to have nightmares a lot as a child apparently. I think that might have been partly behind his interest in the paranormal – you know, confronting his demons." She looked on the verge of saying something else, but stopped, frowning slightly before saying, "Oh, I'm sure he'll be fine. Come on through."

They followed her into the house. Eloise left her bags beside one of the sofas and Will laid his bundle down the centre of the coffee table between them. Chris came in then, with three cups of green tea and a plate of biscuits.

He looked more composed now, but as he put the drinks down and sat next to Rachel, he said, "What's in the bundle?"

"Four swords," said Will.

"Swords?" Chris seemed intrigued, curious, no more than that. "Are you expecting to need them?"

"I have no idea what I expect of the coming days, but the swords were gifted to me in the cathedral."

"You're not going to believe this," said Eloise. "They were given to us by four devils! Like man-sized

31

gargoyles, but with wings. It was so weird."

Rachel was shaking her head, incredulous. But instantly Chris said, "They're in the city?"

Eloise didn't catch the tone of his question and said only, "I know, it's amazing, right there in the cathedral. We thought they'd come to attack us at first."

Will, though, had not been alone in reading a different meaning into Chris's question, or the fear with which it had been laced. Rachel looked at Chris with suspicion, even with a hint of perceived betrayal. Chris's shock had not been at the description of the devils, but their location – he had encountered them before perhaps, and had most likely been dreaming of them ever since.

He seemed to regain his composure though and said, "But you have no idea what the swords are for?"

Will smiled. "Presumably their purpose will become clear soon enough."

Rachel still looked distracted by Chris, but she put a brave face on it and said, "Well, I suppose it's better to have them on your side than against you."

"Indeed," said Will.

But he felt for Rachel, and to some extent he felt sorry for both of them. They had once been so close, and yet now it was painfully apparent that they were on divergent paths. And he could not help but think how much simpler and happier their lives might have been if they had not accidentally filmed him more than two decades ago.

They set off shortly afterwards, into a clear night with a moon that would be full within a few days. There was a slight chill in the air, but nothing to suggest that only three weeks ago the landscape had been swathed in winter. This was almost a spring night, the promise of warmer times threaded within it.

They were all lost in their own thoughts during the journey, but when they reached the school gates, Rachel turned to them and said, "Please don't hesitate to get in touch – it doesn't matter how trivial it is, we're here to help."

Eloise smiled. "You've been so good to us."

Will looked at Chris, who in turn glanced nervously at the woods that shielded the school and the parkland from the road. There it was, this new fear that had been gripping him these last few weeks and disturbing his sleep.

Once they'd been dropped off and had set off up the drive, Will said, "Chris was afraid. He kept looking into the woods."

Eloise looked to either side herself, as if remembering the attack by the crows in this same spot, and said, "Do you see anything out there?"

"No, but I think I know what he was looking for. I

don't think you noticed, but when you described the devils, his tone was that of someone who recognised their description. It was merely their location that shocked him."

"Yes!" She looked at him. "I mean, no, I didn't notice at the time, but now that you mention it. But why would he . . .?" The thoughts assembled in her mind and she said quietly, "You think he saw them here, at Marland."

"I suspect so."

"He's definitely with Wyndham."

"It seems more than likely. I only hope he surprises us yet, because I do believe Chris is a good man."

Even as he said it though, Will knew how much evil had been done throughout history in the cause of good.

They walked on up to the darkened school and Will opened the side door for them and followed Eloise inside. They made their way up in silence, and were only a short distance from her room when Will sensed someone coming.

He tried to stop Eloise, but could not call, and then he noticed torchlight seeping through the darkness towards him as Eloise walked round a corner in front of him.

"Oh, good God!" It was a man's voice and it was immediately apparent that Eloise's sudden appearance had frightened him.

Eloise seemed unperturbed and laughed a little as she

said, "Oh, Mr Asquith, I'm so sorry. I didn't mean to startle you."

Will stayed back, ready to slip away further.

"Eloise? You frightened the life out of me. What are you doing at . . ." He regained his composure quickly and said, "Sorry, of course. How's your aunt? Your cousin told me about her being sick again when she came to collect your things."

"Much better, thank you. In fact, it's my cousin who just dropped me off. I didn't turn the lights on because I didn't want to disturb anyone."

"Of course, of course." He sounded bookish, and his tone was relaxed. But then he said, "How did you get in?"

Without skipping a beat, Eloise said, "The side door was open. My cousin called Dr Higson today, so maybe he left it open."

"Er, possibly, only, I'm sure . . ." He came to a stop and said, "Oh, ignore me. Things have been a little strange lately, what with Alex Shawcross disappearing, then Marcus running away and being found . . . well, you know. Let me escort you back to your room."

"Thank you."

Their steps and the torchlight drifted away and Will followed at a distance, carrying the swords and Eloise's larger bag – fortunately, Mr Asquith hadn't noticed her lack of luggage. Will found it even more extraordinary that he was willing to accept Eloise's mysterious return like this, but then perhaps all the staff were under instructions from Dr Higson that Eloise could come and go as she pleased.

There was something else at play too, because Mr Asquith had been very understated in saying that things had been a little strange lately. First, there had been Marcus's death, the end of the bright future Wyndham had promised his mother by bringing him to Marland. No one knew that he'd been selected by Wyndham as a spy, or that his death had been indirectly related to him changing allegiance, attaching himself to the very people he'd been intended to undermine.

As far as most people were concerned, a boy brought in on a full scholarship, rescued from poverty and a troubled background, had simply reverted to type. He'd been killed in a fall during an act of arson, that was the official line, and it grieved Will that the life of such an honourable and bright boy had been so maligned.

So on its own, the death of Marcus might have been easily explained away. But coupled with the disappearance of Alex Shawcross, an accomplished student from a wealthy family, it amounted to something more, and the staff probably felt the entire school was slipping out of control. Would it take much

36

more before parents started to remove their children?

Mr Asquith left Eloise at her door with the words, "Good to have you back, Eloise," and continued on his nervous rounds. Will kept his distance until he was sure Asquith had gone, but then approached and gently knocked on the door. As she opened it, the lamp was on, but covered with a scarf.

She smiled and said, "That was close." She ushered Will in, closed the door behind him, then took the bag and put it on the floor at the bottom of the bed. She gestured for him to sit down and then sat on the bed herself. "It'll be odd, sleeping without knowing you're watching me."

"I'll be thinking of you, if that helps."

Eloise smiled again. "Where will you go tonight?"

He looked round her room, at the single bed, the desk with its lamp, the posters and the books on the shelves. It was her little world and he wished he could stay here with her, as much as he knew it was impossible. This was an intimate space, warm and human, and he belonged elsewhere, in the dark and the cold, in the abandoned night.

"I'll visit the new house, and I may stay there tonight, but I prefer the chapel here, I think."

"So do I. It means you're close by. I can come and see you."

He didn't bother arguing the point, but said only, "I should go, and you should sleep."

She laughed. "But I only woke up a couple of hours ago." The implication seemed to be clear, that she would much rather go with him wherever he was going.

He stood up. "Eloise, we have been away three weeks, and we know not what has happened in that time. Allow me tonight to check the new house, to check the school."

"But . . ." Something in his expression convinced her to give up and she said, "OK, I suppose I'll read, but don't do anything exciting without me."

"I'll try not to."

He smiled and left, walking quickly and carefully down through the school. He didn't encounter Mr Asquith again, but the teacher had locked the side door. Will opened it again and closed the lock behind him, then set off across the parkland towards the new house.

The moonlight was uncomfortable on his skin, the pale disc burning a hole in the night sky. The weather was set fair for the days ahead and yet he would rather have it overcast. Ahead he could see the stand of trees that obscured the two houses from each other, and to his eyes it was as visible as a lit city street, so bright was the moon.

And then he stopped walking and listened. Because

beyond those trees, quite unmistakably, he could hear someone running. He couldn't see them yet, but someone was there, and there was no doubt about it, the person Will could hear was running straight towards him.

6

It was a girl. He still couldn't see her, but he could hear her rapid, fearful breathing. Suddenly she came hurtling round the stand of trees, almost losing her footing on the dewy grass, but not slowing down. She was running directly into his path now.

Will could already see that she was fair-haired and that she was wearing the Marland Abbey uniform with a dark coat over it, which flew behind her as she ran. He thought of moving to the side, out of her path, certain that it was still dark enough and that she was afraid enough not to notice him.

But the thought came too late. She saw or sensed him standing there. She let out a small scream and kept running, but called out, "Who's there?" When he didn't respond she tried to stop herself, but she had too much momentum and the park sloped down slightly to where Will was standing, so for all her efforts, she careered headlong into him.

She let out another little scream, but he caught her

with his free arm and said quickly, "Don't worry, you're safe. You're safe now." The words were well chosen because he didn't think this girl had spooked herself – she was running from something.

Almost at once, his words – or perhaps the tone of his voice – had a calming effect on her, and she said quickly in a whisper, "Thank God, thank God. Who are you? What house?"

He took in the scent of her, healthy and vital, and was relieved that he did not need blood. "Never mind that – what are you running from?"

That set her fear racing again and she looked urgently over her shoulder. She probably couldn't see, but Will knew nothing was pursuing her.

"I don't know. I saw, maybe I didn't see, but I know something was there, and it was coming towards me . . ." She backed away a step, staring hopelessly at Will in the darkness, and her tone was tense and suspicious as she said, "Who are you? You didn't say. They'd hear me scream from here, at the school." She kept backing away.

"You have nothing to fear from me." Again the sound of his voice seemed to calm her and she at least stopped moving. He had little choice in the matter now, and said, "My name's Will, and I'm not at the school. I'll escort you back there if you like, and I can assure you that if anyone has followed you, I will protect you from them."

Her eyes had perhaps adjusted because she saw the bundle in his hand and said, "What are you carrying? You're not a metal thief, are you?"

Her tone reminded him of Eloise, that same confidence and forthrightness even after being so recently terrified – it was probably something instilled by the school.

"I am not a thief of any kind. But I have given you my name and you have not given me yours."

"Sorry, how terribly rude of me. Sophie. Sophia actually, but everyone calls me Sophie. I . . ."

Will put up his hand to stop her because as she'd spoken he had seen her pursuer emerge from around the stand of trees, at a canter rather than the gallop of the chase. He could see that it was one of her classmates, suggesting a malicious prank, and was concerned only because it meant he would have been seen by two pupils in one night.

"Don't be afraid, but here comes your attacker, and it's a boy from your own school."

She looked momentarily alarmed, then outraged, and finally confused as she turned and squinted up the park. She could see and perhaps also hear the boy running lightly down the gentle slope towards them, but could not make him out in detail.

"How on earth can you tell he's from the school?"

Will guessed Sophie was in the same year as Eloise, but the boy running towards them looked a couple of years below, an impish quality about him. He wore the uniform, but without a coat. He was laughing silently too, and continued to laugh even as he saw their shadows ahead of him.

He was close enough now that Sophie was able to say, "Oh, you're right, it is our uniform." Was it the blue and white striped collar, Will wondered, floating above the darker green of the boy's sweater. Sounding fierce, she said, "You are in so much trouble! Who are you?"

The boy stopped maybe half a dozen paces short of them, and though he continued to laugh silently, he didn't answer her. Sophie took a torch from her overcoat pocket – Will realised that he would have to find out what she'd been doing out there – and pointed it at the boy as she turned it on.

To Will's eyes, the boy's face became dazzling, a white disc as bright as the moon, big dark eyes, messy brown hair, much like many of the other boys in the school.

Sophie said, "Why don't you answer . . ." She stopped short, unsure of herself again, her confidence melting away. "Who are you?"

The boy gave a sort of incredulous smile, but still did not answer, a continued silence that was unsettling in some way.

Will said, "What's wrong?"

Sophie kept her torch on the boy and didn't even turn her face from him as she said, "He's wearing our uniform, but I've never seen that boy before. He's not in our school."

"He looks younger than you, perhaps you just haven't encountered him."

"No, I would know." As if to prove it, she asked the same question she'd addressed to Will, saying, "What house are you in?"

The boy still only laughed, but even as the question had been asked, Will had been disentangling the scents around him – the girl, the parkland, the night air – and he knew now that whatever faint scent was coming from this boy, it wasn't human.

He loosened his bundle enough to draw one of the swords and said, "Stand back, Sophie."

He ran forward, and as he lunged with the sword, the boy mutated violently in front of him, as quickly as if someone had flicked a switch. It was visible only for a moment before Will's sword struck, a creature the like of which he'd never seen, as much like a black insect as anything else, fanged and horned.

Will heard Sophie cry out some word or other, but that noise was drowned out by a piercing shriek as his sword cleaved the thing in two. It melted instantly into the ground, then a second later re-emerged, the two halves formed into perfect smaller versions of the creature Will had just slain.

One ran at him, the other for the girl. But Will was too quick, thrusting the blade into one, crippling it, before swinging round, covering his eyes against Sophie's torch beam, and slicing the sword down on to the thing as it scuttled towards her.

It melted into the ground as before. Will turned back to where the first creature appeared to be remoulding itself. He swung the sword hard, cracking through shell or bone, through the soft body parts, until his blade hit the grass and the creature soaked away into the earth.

Will edged back a few paces, urging Sophie to do the same with little more than a hand gesture. He studied the ground in front of them, and her instinct was to do the same because she ran her torch beam across the grass again and again. It was her torch beam too that caught it, a shape forming, pulsing under the ground.

"There!"

Will stepped forward and drove the blade into the ground. Another muffled shriek before the resistance melted away. He pulled the sword free and stepped back again. But this time there was nothing to be seen. Instead, Will could feel the ground moving beneath

45

them, as if some serpent was burrowing away towards the new house.

And when it did emerge again, it was too far from them for Will to attack. It was back to full size, appeared to get its bearings, then snapped back into the boy, still laughing. It snapped again, flipping up into the air, landing as a white hare, which stared at them for a moment or two, with the same big dark eyes, and then leapt away towards the distant woodland.

Will watched the creature bounding away and then saw the torch beam wobble and heard the torch itself fall to the floor behind him. He turned, carefully picking it up and switching it off. Sophie was still staring into the middle distance, her expression like someone with mild amnesia.

"What? What do you . . .? It . . ."

"It's gone now, whatever it was."

She didn't turn away so he moved round her. In the heat of the attack she'd seemed to handle the shock, but it had caught up with her now. Her face was frozen and drained of blood, her eyes fixed on something unseen.

Gently, he said, "Sophie?"

Without any suggestion of knowing what she was saying, words stuttered out of her mouth. "That . . . what would it . . . How? What was it?"

He was so used to Eloise, who even at the beginning

46

had dealt almost serenely with everything thrown at her, that this girl's traumatised reaction had caught him off guard. Nor did he have the time to explain these things to her, if they could even be explained.

Will glanced behind, making sure the creature was not returning. It had shared some of the same characteristics as the spirits Wyndham had summoned back in November, but this had been something different, he knew it. And though he'd never experienced anything quite like it before, he knew enough of myths and legends to have an idea.

He presumed they'd just encountered a shapeshifter. He'd read about people who'd come across such intangible creatures in remote country, often attributed as meetings with the god Pan. And looking at Sophie now, he even understood why the word panic had arisen out of such encounters, because she still did not look far from being frightened to death.

He felt now that he only had one option. He stepped closer, staring into her eyes, and though she was still in shock and had only moonlight by which to see him, she saw enough to be hooked and drawn into his world. She tried to speak again and he reached up and put his finger on the warm softness of her lips.

"Sophie, you hear me and only me. I am Will and I am your friend. You need not worry about that creature.

It was only a shapeshifter. You accept all these things as if you always knew about them. You have no fear. You have no desire to talk to anyone but me about them. These are our secrets. And now it's time for me to walk you back to the school. Would you like that?"

As he spoke, he saw the trauma falling away from her, her expression relaxing. He released her and she nodded and stared at him quizzically, a smile forming on her lips as she said, "Sorry, I didn't hear, what did you just say?"

"I said, would you like me to walk you back to the school?"

"That's terribly kind, Will. Not that I mind walking back alone, but . . ." She sounded casual and light-hearted as she said, "Why do you think it came after me? It was a shapeshifter, wasn't it? At least I think that's what it was. Odd that it should appear just like that, don't you think?"

Even influenced by his hypnotism, it was a pertinent question. It was possible of course that this was something summoned by Wyndham, but everything the sorcerer had so far brought forth had focused its energies on Will or Eloise, not on random strangers. Will doubted Wyndham would have wasted his own energies so recklessly.

Something else was happening though, something beyond Wyndham's meddling. Will thought of the

48

devils in the cathedral, of the gift of swords, the tribute of gold. Was the shapeshifter part of the same process? Was it possible that, whatever had happened in the last three weeks, the barriers between this world and the underworld were breaking down? If so, then surely devils and shapeshifters would be but the beginning of it.

7

I spoke of knowing everything, but that isn't entirely true. I do not know where the Grykken came from, only what was said of it. Some said it had fallen from the sky, some that it had emerged from the underworld itself, from the very depths of the cavern in which it lived.

What I do know is that the Grykken had lived beneath that mountain for as long as people had spoken their history. Perhaps it had been there since before the ice retreated, for this is a northern land of which I speak. Before people were settled in that country, before those people had kings, the Grykken lived there.

None had ever seen it out of its lair, and the people of the northern kingdoms might have lived happily in ignorance of its existence were it not for the gold to be found in abundance beneath the mountain. So plentiful was the gold, it could almost be pulled from the rock with bare hands, and no danger, no monster, would be enough to deter men from the search for such treasure.

That many of them failed to come back was of little consequence when set against the huge hauls obtained by those who did return. What did the Grykken look like? All had different views, but all agreed it was a thing of darkness, too vast and too fast to be seen in its entirety.

All agreed its skin was as black as the deepest parts of those caverns, but some said it was like a snake, others that it was armour-plated like a monstrous beetle. All agreed that it had claws and fangs sharper than any sword, but some said it had three heads, some that it had four.

The worst fate belonged to those who escaped the clutches of the Grykken, but with a blood wound for their trouble. These men always fell sick and died, but their bodies would not burn and though they were buried, they rose again, some within a matter of months, some after many years.

These revenants wreaked havoc among the people with whom they had once lived. Very soon it became common practice to decapitate the wounded as soon as they died.

But miners were not to be its only victims. In the days of the first kings, the story of the Grykken had already spread, and heroes would be drawn from near and far to set themselves against the unseen monster.

Many of those heroes too did not return; many more met the crueller fate. Others returned unharmed, traces of scalding and noxious blood still on their swords, but none could claim complete victory.

Then came the reign of Sivard, a hero of great renown. The good king's cousin challenged him to destroy the Grykken and in a rare moment of folly, Sivard promised he would do so. Certain death awaited, he was sure of that, but then his seer told him that victory would be his, that three more kings would come to assist him, all would be injured, but in overcoming the Grykken they would escape its evil curse and take its power for themselves.

Sivard bided his time, and it was as the seer had said. First came a king from the distant east, Xiang Xi, crossing the snow-swept wastes with a caravan of a thousand retainers. Then Archelaos came from the south, bearing gifts of gold and jewels enough to fill twelve caskets.

Sivard welcomed them, but though they were eager to test themselves against the fabled Grykken, he insisted they wait. And at last, from the haunted lands to the west, came Lorcan Labraid, a warrior king of fearsome reputation.

Labraid had his own seer with him, a witch who foretold what would come to pass. The four kings would need to enter the cavern together, she said. Each would sever one of the Grykken's four heads, ensuring that they could not grow back and thereby bringing about the creature's demise. But, she warned, the Grykken's power would only become theirs if they received a blood wound in the battle.

Sivard gave a great feast the night before their desperate venture, the like of which was not seen again for many centuries. As young as the king was, he was wise enough to know that his seer and Labraid's witch were not infallible, and that by next evening four kingdoms might be without their protectors.

Then the morning came and the four brave warriors descended into the mountainous lair, Sivard at their head, as befitted the host of this expedition. And as they hoped and dreaded, deep within the dark, they encountered the beast, their flaming torches managing only to illuminate glimpses of its shining black flanks, the flashing white of fang and claw.

They set to. Sivard struck first, as was his right, and was very nearly the first to perish. As he ran at the creature's head, a claw with razor sharp talons swiped at him. Sivard jumped backwards, almost escaping, receiving only a gash along his left cheek – nothing to a warrior of his standing, but it would be enough to rob him of his life if they did not succeed in their quest.

Without taking pause, Sivard pushed forward again and struck at the neck of the Grykken, which let out a terrible shriek. Lorcan Labraid saw no reason to stand on ceremony. His torch caught a glimpse of another head, seeking to persecute brave Sivard, and Labraid struck fierce and strong, severing the head with a single sweep of his sword.

Xiang Xi and Archelaos set themselves against the other heads. Almost immediately, Xiang Xi received a deep gash across his chest, but he only fought on all the harder, knowing that death would be his anyway unless they triumphed. Archelaos too was wounded, the creature lashing out and biting his shoulder, so violently that he lost his grip on the sword in his hand, leaving it embedded in the creature's neck.

Lorcan Labraid ran to his side, and set about finishing the task of removing the last of the four heads, moving too quickly for the venomous fangs that lashed and tore through the darkness. His job was almost done, the neck almost severed, when Labraid realised he alone had received no blood wound.

Sivard and Xiang Xi approached with flaming torches to aid the stricken Archelaos, and those lights illuminated the last of the creature's heads. So too, it was Labraid alone who stared into the Grykken's fathomless eyes, he alone who understood the nature of *this beast. Even with that wicked knowledge, he raised his free arm, inviting the monster to lock its fangs round it, which the desperate creature did.*

Ignoring the pain that tore through him, fearless Labraid completed the task of severing its neck. The head remained gripped to his bloodied arm, the jaws locked so tight that it took all the strength of Sivard, Labraid and Xiang Xi to remove it. They thought to take the final head back to the surface as a trophy, but as they stood assessing their own injuries, the entire carcass became consumed by a blue flame, illuminating the vast gold-filled cavern.

How long had their battle taken? They did not know. It had seemed a strenuous fight and yet none of them was left weary now. They stayed for a while by the torchlight and talked over what had taken place there, and with great surprise, they saw little by little, even as they talked, that their wounds healed.

Even Archelaos, who had seemed so critically injured, was soon recovered enough to declare himself fit for more. These were the promised powers they had sought in their battle, coming on more quickly than any of them had imagined.

Other changes were also afoot. They imagined themselves only wishing to savour their victory in private, but it was not by chance that they stayed in that deep cavern until the sun had slipped across the western horizon.

Darkness had fallen complete by the time they finally emerged. Their retainers, their thanes and followers awaited them there, certain their masters had all met their deaths.

And when the four men emerged into the night, still bearing their swords and their dying torches, a deafening cheer filled the heavens. There was jubilation, but none yet knew that the four kings who had just returned from the place of death were not the same four kings who had gone there. The Grykken was dead, but what the Grykken had been still lived on in these four heroes.

8

As they set off walking, Will asked, "How did you plan to get back into the school?"

"One of the windows in the Heston common room doesn't lock properly."

"I see."

Sophie was carefree now, as if they'd always known each other, as if they'd had a perfectly normal evening. Will didn't know how long the spell would last though, or how much of the trauma would seep back into her as it wore off.

"And do you mind telling me what you were doing at the new house at this time of night?"

"Promise me you won't . . ." She stopped. "No, I don't need you to promise. How terribly strange. We've only just met and I still don't really know who you are, yet I trust you entirely."

"I feel the same way about you." Will felt a little guilty for earning that trust under false pretences, and for the time being, as long as Sophie was within his power, he

57

didn't need to worry about whether or not he could trust her. But she hadn't acted like one of Wyndham's agents, not least in that she had allowed herself to be hypnotised in the first place.

She sounded freshly forlorn as she said, "A friend of mine went missing a few weeks ago. He was in Heston House too. I knew he was going out somewhere, but he wouldn't say where. I saw him all dressed up in black and I made some joke about him looking like a spy. Anyway, he said, 'Well, you could say it was something of national importance, and you'll have to trust me on that,' which at the time seemed terribly strange."

She was talking about Alex Shawcross, that much was clear, the boy Will had found ransacking the gift shop in the new house, the boy whose bloodless body now lay in a makeshift coffin somewhere in the labyrinth.

"I don't understand."

"Nor did I until yesterday. Alex – that's his name – still hasn't been found and I wondered if that strange comment of his was all about the words 'national' and 'trust', so I decided to go up there and take a look around. Wish I hadn't now." She glanced behind. "Maybe that shapeshifter took him."

"Sophie, if he has disappeared, can you not see how foolish it was to go to the new house on your own? Who knows what danger you could have been walking into."

She looked as if she wanted to say something, but her thoughts ran up against the limits he'd set around her. She walked a couple of paces in confused silence and then said, "It was stupid, I know. When I said he's a friend, well, he is, but I suppose I have a bit of a crush on him, or a lot of a crush, and I think he likes me too, although he's a lot older than me." Will smiled at the concept of one or two years constituting an insurmountable age gap, but it was an amusement that was tinged with sadness on many levels. "Everyone thinks he's run away, but I think he's dead. I just know it."

"So why are you looking for him?"

"I want to know what's happened. Wouldn't you?"

They were almost at the school and Will was quieter as he said, "Perhaps I would, but I hope you've learned now that it is not safe to do as you did tonight."

"I have, and really, I'm so terribly grateful you came along when you did."

They walked round the school and she approached a window. In darkness beyond was the common room that Eloise and Marcus had looked at contemptuously just a month earlier. Sophie pulled the window open and then turned.

"Thanks, Will. I hope I'll see you around."

"I'm sure you will," he said, though in truth he doubted it.

59

But then she looked at him and laughed and said, "I just had the strangest thought."

"What is it?"

"I don't know why, but as I looked at you just now . . ." She shook her head before adding, "Last year, I went to a clairvoyant, completely stupid, full of meaningless drivel that anyone could use to suit themselves. But for some reason, one of the things she said came into my mind when I just looked at you."

"And what was it?"

"Oh, ridiculous. It was the last thing she said, and she repeated it like two or three times – you need the boy, the boy needs you. Like I said, drivel." Sophie laughed and then climbed with remarkable grace through the window, leaning out briefly to say, "Goodnight, Will."

"Goodnight," he said as she lowered the window.

He didn't move though, watching instead as she crossed the darkened room and disappeared through a doorway. This girl had experienced something extraordinary tonight, the kind of thing that, without Will's powers to lessen the blow, might have traumatised her indefinitely. Yet it was Will who was left in confusion, his thoughts tumbling violently.

Why had she used that expression? For the briefest moment he wondered if everything he'd believed over the last four months had been a fantasy. Jex had talked of him needing the girl, the girl needing him, and Eloise's picture had been in the notebook, Jex had given her the medallion, Will had found her.

Despite all of that, could it be possible that Eloise was not the girl Jex had spoken of? The witches had used that same expression specifically in relation to Eloise, but by their own admission, their interest was in Eloise rather than in Will or his destiny.

Will had felt from the beginning that there was a connection between them, but was that little more than him being smitten with Eloise? Perhaps, by the same token, Sophie had originally imagined the clairvoyant's words as a reference to Alex Shawcross because that's who she'd wanted to need her.

Will started walking, back across the park, heading to the new house, a troubled and complex argument playing out in his head. Too many coincidences had linked him to Eloise, but that could speak both of destiny and of some sort of entrapment.

Could *Eloise* be working for Wyndham? No! He smothered the thought immediately, ashamed that it could have occurred to him at all. Besides, Wyndham had attacked her. She was true, he knew it, but could it be possible that she was not the girl he needed to fulfil his destiny? Could it be possible that the girl spoken of in the prophecies was not Eloise but Sophie, who had been here at Marland all this time?

Will stopped for a moment, wanting to turn back, to find Sophie and ask her questions, discover who she was and what she knew, whether she realised she knew it or not. Equally, he wanted to go back and speak to Eloise, to tell her what had happened and see her response.

But he walked on again, certain that this doubting was madness. He had known from the start that Eloise was a part of his story, and if he had been wrong about that, if his destiny was to be without her, he'd rather return to the earth right now and come back in another lifetime.

He cleared the stand of trees, no longer even sure what he was going to the new house for. He'd wanted to check that nothing had changed in the weeks he'd been away, that the labyrinth was as he'd left it, but it was already clear that so much had changed.

There was the house though, dark against the illuminated night sky. It had been an act of madness on Sophie's part to come out here on her own, yet it was exactly the kind of thing Eloise would also have done. Will had been there to save her of course, and yet if she had come another month or so from now, meeting Will might have meant the end of her life, just as it had done for Alex Shawcross.

He was almost at the house, and with a memory of

the last time they'd been here, of the ghosts wandering about the rooms, the young lady who perhaps had looked down on them from the lit window above, he almost expected a light to turn on now. But there was only stillness, a stillness that was like a presence in itself.

Will had nothing to fear here. He had nothing to fear for himself in any of this. Yet all the same, he found himself reluctant to continue, even as his mind set to work on the lock, as he opened the door and stepped inside.

9

Will made his way quickly through the house to the library and opened the secret entrance down to the labyrinth. The lights were still on – the remnants of Wyndham's trickery – and Will wondered idly if the sorcerer kept them alight with magic or if the National Trust would be met with a huge and inexplicable electricity bill come the spring.

Will idly flicked the switch back and forth a couple of times, but the lights remained on. Then he descended the steps and walked quickly until he reached the beginning of the ruined labyrinth. He didn't think the walls had been moved since, and nor did he sense that anyone else had been here this last month.

He walked along, paying more attention than before to the mass of strange paintings that adorned the walls, to the runic writing, but above all to the creatures depicted there. There were many that could have matched the devils in the cathedral, and others that might have been the fierce, strange insect-monster he'd encountered in the park above. He also noticed something he had never seen before, that animals resembling hares were represented often among the fantastical menagerie.

Will turned into a long tunnel and stopped, knowing that the makeshift coffin containing the body of Alex Shawcross was at the far end of it. His death had tested Will's bond with Eloise, but for the girl he'd met this evening it would have been even more horrifying, to know that the person who'd saved her was also the person responsible for Alex's death, a boy she imagined herself in love with. If Will did need Sophie in some way, it was vital she never discovered that truth.

He took in the air, the faint smell of dry decomposition, the body slowly mummifying, then turned and headed back to the library. He closed the door at the top of the steps, then the other into the first secret passage. The library was still and dark.

He left it behind and strolled through the other downstairs rooms. They were all empty of course, all unchanged. Then, for some unknown reason, he looked at the ceiling above him. He'd heard no noise, could detect no other scent, but he felt compelled to check the upstairs rooms.

He headed back into the hall and started up the stairs, and though he couldn't think why, he felt a sense of anticipation, maybe even dread. He had nothing to fear here, certainly not devils or spirits or shapeshifters. Even so, he made sure that the sword he'd used earlier would be easy to withdraw from the bundle.

Will walked along the main landing, looking into each of the rooms, expecting to be met by . . . something, yet finding nothing. The rooms to the front of the house were bathed in moonlight and as he reached one large bedroom, rather than just look in, he stepped inside.

He crossed to the window and looked down on to the lawns below. Immediately he knew which room this was. He thought back to the last time they'd been here, to the spirit of the young lady they'd seen laughing at a dinner party, who'd also stared with such concern at Will. A silhouette of that same spirit, he was sure, had appeared in this window, looking down at them where they'd stood at a safe distance, before the last of the lights had been extinguished.

That haunting had been Wyndham's work of course, but the spirit of that lady had seemed to act independently of the magic in some way, just as the spirit of Will's mother had when summoned by Fairburn. And the young lady had watched them from here, a room to which Will had found himself drawn.

He turned and walked round the large bedroom, looking at the four-poster bed, the other furniture, a door into a large dressing room. Opposite the bed there was a bureau of some sort with a mirror hanging on the wall above it, and he walked over and opened each of the drawers and compartments, but of course, they were all empty – no one had lived in this house for half a century.

He looked up, trying to think of what it was he was looking for, and then he saw her, or rather her reflection, standing a little way behind him in the mirror, a look of terrible concern and sadness on her face.

He spun round instantly, his eyes still a little dazzled by the moonlight, but there was no one standing there. Just as quickly, he turned back to the mirror, but there was no longer anyone there either. Will had seen her though, it had been the same young woman – it couldn't have been a vision of his own making, he was certain of it.

He turned slowly again and said, "Please, I ask of you, show yourself." The room remained defiantly quiet, and he felt a little foolish to be engaging in conversation with it. Nevertheless, he added, "I am William of Mercia, I am of your family and I believe you have something to tell me, or you would not have appeared as you have."

Still there was nothing. He faced the bureau once more, even opening the drawers again in the hope of repeating the same process. Reluctantly then, he headed slowly for the door and was almost through it when he heard some small noise from the dressing room.

He crossed the room quickly, opening the door. The dressing room too was empty. He stepped inside, trying to see what might have been moved to make the noise, hoping that in itself might be part of some message, but no item was even on display, only the heavy furniture of another age.

Will stepped back into the bedroom and stopped. For she now stood exactly where he'd been at the bureau, her head bowed, as if waiting for him. He edged forward slowly and stopped a few paces from her.

She looked up, staring at him in the reflection just as he had done with her a few moments before. Her face had an immediate familiarity, and not just because he had seen her spirit a month before. In one sense she was typical of the pretty young women of class who'd populated his world a century or two ago, except of course this young lady was also distantly related to him.

She looked directly at him, with the same sad concern as before, and said, "I appear to have misplaced my journals. They were here in the bureau and now they are gone."

"I don't understand."

"You who have known so much," she said with a little smile. "The journals must surely help you, if we could but find them."

Will nodded. "I'll look for them, but pray, who are

you and what is your involvement in this?"

She turned slowly, still with the slight wry smile that did not mask her sadness as she said, "I am not here, Sir. Can it be that I was never here?"

She walked towards him and Will could only stand and watch her advance. As real and solid as she looked, he did not move from her path even as she reached the point of colliding with him. But she walked through him, his vision distorting, the energy fizzing and popping through his body.

Then from behind him, he heard her voice again, saying, "Beware your heart – it is your weakness."

He turned, but she was no longer there.

Will didn't stop to ponder on her appearance here tonight or on the few things she'd said. He returned instead to the bureau, checking what he already knew and what the spirit had confirmed, that all the drawers and compartments were empty.

He walked along the landing then, to the other wing where several of the upstairs rooms had been emptied of whatever had furnished them and filled with display cases to exhibit many of the family's smaller items and collections. From the few brief tours he'd already made, Will seemed to remember it had been mainly jewellery and miniatures, a case of small children's toys, another of ivory ornaments. But he remembered one case displaying a number of books and he made for it now.

A few of the books were volumes written by members of the family, a few more were diaries, but there at the far end, quite tucked away in the corner of a room, were two thick leather-bound journals beneath a print of a young lady, the lady with whom he'd just conversed.

Her name was Harriet Heston-Dangrave and the short text described her as a free-spirited woman who'd toured extensively in Scandinavia and central and eastern Europe. The journals had been kept as records of both her travels and her academic pursuits, and included sketches of historical sights, the locations of which, "sadly", were not known.

One of the journals was open inside the display case, a couple of pages of dense script broken up by a skilfully executed sketch of a mountain pass. Will opened the case and removed the two volumes. Carefully, he looked through the pages and stopped as he reached detailed diagrams of a labyrinth. She'd copied some of the drawings from the walls too, but there was nothing written to indicate where this labyrinth was.

Will was amused by that. Scholars had most likely looked at these diagrams and tried to decipher where she had seen this ancient and mysterious structure. They'd probably retraced the route of her travels, searching for the most likely spots, and it had never occurred to them that this labyrinth was right here, that Harriet had needed to travel no further than a secret passage in the family library to get there.

He saw that she had also made attempts to translate the runic writing from the walls, and there were pages upon pages of notes on the various possible meanings she attached to it all. Even from the snippets Will read standing there in the moonlight, he could understand her fascination – Harriet Heston-Dangrave had known, intuitively or through some gleaned fact, that this mystery was her family's mystery.

Will slipped the books into his overcoat pocket, intent on reading them at leisure. He then went down to the library and selected two aged volumes that could take the place of the journals in the display case, to satisfy the cursory inspections of the house that would still be the norm for another month, till preparations began for the Easter reopening.

He left then, working the lock closed behind him, and setting off across the lawns. He could easily have stayed in the new house, it was true, but he associated those cellars with such torment, and even for one night, he preferred to return to the chapel crypt beneath the school.

He'd only walked a dozen paces from the house when something, he didn't even know what, made him think of putting on his dark glasses, even though he was

71

reasonably accustomed to the moon by now. He started to move his bundle of swords to his left hand, freeing up the right to reach into his pocket for the glasses, but he had not even completed the manoeuvre when there was a brief buzzing, like a surge of electricity, and lights burst out of the darkness, the pain scorching through his eyes.

He shut them tight, gritted his teeth and tried not to scream even in this remote spot. He dropped the swords and fumbled in his pocket for the glasses. And all the time he was trying to think what might be happening here, what he had to do next to protect himself. The only thing he knew for certain was that this was Wyndham's work.

He heard another noise, like a cable snapping, and heard it whoosh towards him. He turned, desperately trying to work out what it was, but in the midst of all that pain he thought too slowly, reacted too slowly, and he understood only as the metal bolt pounded into his chest, tore through the bone and muscle, penetrated his heart. Too late.

He tried to reach up with his last vestige of strength to remove the bolt, but his powers had fallen away from him instantly. He thought for a moment that his arms were still moving, but then realised his legs had buckled and he was falling to the floor.

He crashed down on to the grass, flat on his back,

the energy leaving him so totally that it felt as if he was dissolving into the ground itself. He lay there and opened his eyes a little, looking up at the stars, faint against the power of the moon. And pinned like that, like a butterfly to a board, he awaited his fate.

10

He lay for only a short while, perhaps only seconds, before the lights died. The darkness fell so abruptly that for a moment even Will was unable to see. Quickly though, his eyes adjusted again to the moonlight. His skin prickled under it too.

That prickling discomfort was the only sensation Will had to remind him that he was still attached to his own body. His powers had so completely fallen away from him that he was hardly aware of his limbs and only had some indistinct sense of the pressure from the metal bolt that pierced his heart.

His other senses were still acute, and he waited for the sound or scent of Wyndham approaching because he expected that imminently. Wyndham would never have dared engage Will in combat on normal terms, but now that he was pinned and defenceless, the sorcerer would be more than happy to complete the execution.

Surely that was it, surely Wyndham would appear from his hiding place and remove Will's head, perhaps even with one of the four swords lying uselessly at his side. With greater dread, Will thought back to the vampires kept imprisoned in Wyndham's basement, and feared that the sorcerer would seek to take him captive rather than kill him.

Whatever Wyndham's plans, he was clearly taking no chances because he did not approach and the minutes ticked by. Will's mind wandered to the warning of Harriet's spirit: "Beware your heart – it is your weakness," bitterly appropriate now.

He thought then of how close he lay to the abbey ruins, how close to those dreams he'd had of walking there in sunlight with Eloise. Yet he would never come any closer to those visions.

"Wyndham!" He thought he called out, but even his voice was weakened and hoarse. There was no response anyway. Will listened, took in the air, and now he began to wonder if Wyndham was even there.

It seemed quite typical of the man that he might have set up an automated trap, much as poachers in an earlier age had set traps and left them. If that was the case, it could still be that an alarm had been triggered, that Wyndham would make his way here in due course, but Will had no idea how long that might be.

He thought of Eloise, not walking among the ruins, but the Eloise of recent memory, of the days spent lying

75

together and talking in his chambers, the Eloise whose kiss he could now remember without the agony and blood-hunger that came with it.

As had been the case since the beginning, since his fight to the death with Asmund, he felt he would be failing her by dying, but for the first time it was beyond his control. There was nothing he could do to save himself now, no inner reserves of strength to call upon.

He'd been there for as much as an hour and still there was no sound of Wyndham's approach, not even a distant car. Could it be that Wyndham had set this trap, but that he would not come? Will couldn't turn his head, but he sensed the progress of the moon and imagined it would be only another couple of hours before the first glimmer of light appeared on the eastern horizon. That represented a horror of a different order, perhaps even worse than that of being taken prisoner by Wyndham.

He knew that in even the first insipid moments of dawn his skin would begin to burn and blister. Daylight proper, and in particular the touch of the direct sunlight that this clear sky promised, would be nothing less than the fires of hell to him, and no less eternal in their torment. Because one thing he now knew was that sunlight, for all the agony it caused, would not kill him.

And how long would he have to endure it before being discovered? If Wyndham did not come, it was possible

Will could remain here for days without being found, consumed by burning through the daylight hours, his body slowly healing each night, but never quite enough, the damage accumulating with each turn of the earth.

He hated to think what he would resemble by the time he was found. And it was true that, even then, if the caretaker or some other person removed the metal bolt, he would recover his strength soon enough and the burns would heal. But he had seen how crazed those creatures had become in Wyndham's basement and did not doubt that his own mind would also succumb.

None of the possible scenarios was good, and the weight of them pressed down on him as much as his own weakness. Very quickly he had reached the point of not caring what happened, but only wishing it would happen soon.

And then, finally, Will heard movement from off to his right. At first he thought it might be an animal, even as it seemed to approach little by little, hesitantly. His head was tilted slightly in the other direction, so even straining his eyes as far as he could to the right, he could see nothing, not even the tops of the trees.

He listened for the other sounds he might have expected from an animal, grazing, snuffling, the telltale movements, tried to pick up the scents of the animals with which he was familiar – rabbits, badgers, deer. He became certain then that this was no wild animal, and he called out in his now papery voice, "Show yourself. Who are you? Approach."

At first there was no response, but after a few moments more, he detected some kind of movement, as if a watchful approach was being made. The only thing he couldn't understand was that he still picked up no scent. He'd come to the conclusion that whoever it was had to be further away than he'd thought, when quite suddenly a figure appeared, standing over him.

It was that small boy with the large dark eyes, the Marland Abbey uniform. Even now, he laughed as he had before, a silent and oddly vacant laugh as he stared down at Will. It seemed unlikely that the shapeshifter had been responsible for the trap, but it seemed appropriate somehow that this creature should so quickly have its revenge on the one who'd attacked it.

"Do your worst," said Will.

The boy stopped laughing in response, which Will imagined was a sign that it was about to click into another form, but instead, the boy moved around Will, dropped to one knee and pulled the metal bolt from his chest.

The result was instantaneous, as if a massive weight had been lifted from him. Energy surged back through his body, so rapidly that he could feel himself jolting with the shock of it. Without thinking about it, he lifted his hands and felt round the wound on his chest, as if wanting to check that the obstruction had completely vanished.

He sat upright then. The boy had backed away and was staring down at him quizzically. Why had he done this, when Will had treated him as an enemy and visited such violence upon him?

Will looked around, still a little dazed, as he said, "Why . . ." Before he could say any more, the boy flipped backwards into the air, landing again as the winter hare and bounding away to the treeline at the edge of the lawns. The hare flipped again as it reached cover, turning once more into the boy who looked at Will before gesturing for him to follow.

Will saw the bundle of swords nearby and picked them up. He leaned on them as he climbed to his feet, realising that his strength had not yet returned to its former level. Walking across the lawn also took him much longer and required more effort than normal. He could feel his strength building moment by moment, but for the time being, he was very much an invalid.

The boy waited patiently all that time, and retreated further into the cover of the trees only as Will reached him. Once Will was alongside him, he pointed upwards and Will saw there part of the mechanism that had entrapped him.

There were devices attached to the trees, the one above still primed with a bolt for firing. An electronic box of some sort sat below it, but the boy pointed to the cables running down the tree which had now been severed. He pointed to other trees, each similarly armed and similarly disabled.

Will nodded, turned to the boy and said, "This was Wyndham's work. I'll return when my strength is recovered and destroy them properly." The boy smiled, though Will wasn't certain he'd understood him. "Why did you help me? I treated you harshly, for which I'm now sorry, but why did you save me?"

The boy continued to smile without responding further, and at first Will thought he had the confirmation that his words hadn't been understood. Then, quite unexpectedly, the boy gestured to himself and dropped to one knee with his head bowed before standing again.

That was it. As with the devils, this creature, this shapeshifter, had emerged from the underworld. And just as in the labyrinth those countless paintings culminated in an image of Will ruling over all, so now these creatures, even the most monstrous, bowed the knee to him.

Eloise had talked of him being a king and he had dismissed it because he was no king by any definition he had known. Yet in the minds of these creatures he was indeed their sovereign, and he had seen his first glimpse of the kingdom he would rule and the subjects he would govern.

He nodded his understanding to the boy and said, "I take it you have no power of speech?"

The boy shook his head.

"Then I cannot know your name, but I thank you." Will looked up into the sky and said, "I must return to the old house." He walked back out of the trees to the edge of the lawn and started to walk slowly away. He'd only taken a few painfully slow paces though when the boy caught hold of his arm. Will stopped and turned. The boy's large eyes studied him, as if intrigued by Will's continued weakness.

Will said, "My strength will return quickly, but it might take some hours. Don't worry, thanks to your efforts, I am unharmed otherwise."

The boy nodded, took a step back and switched with violent speed, once again becoming the monstrous insect Will had attacked in the park. It was like nothing Will had seen before and he tried to take in the details, but couldn't because instantly it began to bulge and buckle and snapped into a new form.

It was Will who stepped back now because the black horse that stood there towered over him. Its nostrils flared, its eyes focusing on Will, as if in that one feature, that gaze, this creature remained identifiably the same. It lowered its head, and though Will knew this was some other creature, his ancient affinity with horses meant he could not stop himself reaching out a hand to it.

He moved alongside the horse then, patting its flank, and mustered his reserves before jumping up on to it. The horse waited till he was settled, then set off at a gentle canter towards the school, its movement smooth, more fluid than any horse Will had ever ridden.

It headed to the far side of the school before stopping, and at first Will could not understand what had taken it there. Then he realised that this was the closest point to the chapel. Will hadn't mentioned the crypt. It was possible the creature understood that he would want the chapel, that his kind always did, but Will wondered if the shapeshifter had come here because it was linked to the chapel itself in some way.

Marcus Jenkins had told them that Wyndham's powers did not work there. Could this be the reason, that the chapel itself provided a gateway to the underworld? Another memory lurched into his mind, of Edgar, the sad and honourable vampire imprisoned by Wyndham. Will had told him about the gateway being blocked, but Edgar had insisted, saying, *No, you have been there, you know it.* He had seemed deranged at the time, but was it possible this was what he'd meant, that there was another gateway outside the labyrinth and this was it?

Will lowered himself from the horse and looked up at the darkened school, wondering now about the decision to build the house on this spot. He'd always imagined it had been a desire to build some small distance away from the confiscated abbey itself, but perhaps there had been more to it.

He turned, subconsciously prepared to pat the horse again, but found the boy standing there. He smiled, the mischievous smile Will had first seen in the park, then jumped into the air and tumbled into a flurry of wings, transformed instantly into a large owl. It swooped away, then flew past close and low before arcing away into the night sky.

At the same time, Will could hear the distant noise of a car approaching the new house. His immediate assumption was that Wyndham had finally arrived, too late for his moment of triumph, and soon he would be cursing that he'd been so far away. If Will hadn't been weakened, he would have rushed back there himself, to end the sorcerer's interference once and for all. Instead, he carried his bundle of swords and walked slowly to the door to the school kitchens. He still felt alarmingly weak, but there was much to do before the dawn, and certainly before he saw Eloise again.

He had imagined his return to Marland as the first

hesitant step back towards his future. He'd had little idea of how he'd proceed, but it seemed now that something had happened in the last few weeks, that the wheels had been set in motion, with or without him, and that he had returned to Marland not a moment too soon.

11

In what little time he had left before the school stirred into life, Will made a quick exploration of the chapel, then descended into the crypt and searched its two main rooms more thoroughly than he had on his previous visit. He was searching for an entrance to another chamber and knew from his own hiding place beneath the cathedral that it would be well-hidden.

Still he found nothing that even suggested a likely opening. As a final measure, he decided to investigate the tombs themselves, but he heard a car approaching somewhere in the world above, then voices, perhaps the school's cooks coming in to start the breakfast preparations, and he decided to leave that part of his search until the following night. He didn't want to take anything apart that couldn't be quickly restored if someone came to the crypt.

Instead, he unlocked the ossuary door, ready to retreat to that further hiding place if it seemed he might be disturbed here, then settled down on the floor with his bundle of swords and took out the two leather-bound journals from his overcoat pocket. Rather than open them though, he placed them on the floor next to him and unbuttoned his shirt to look at his injury. The puncture wound had been small and neat and had already greatly healed. It would probably leave less of a scar than he'd inflicted upon himself with a wooden stake all those years ago.

On that occasion of course, the stake had been pulled free while Will had been in the depths of a hibernating sleep, so he had no way of knowing how long it had taken for his strength to return to its normal levels. Consequently, he did not know how long it would take now. He felt stronger with each passing hour, but was still conscious of not being yet returned to his full capabilities. If he was attacked now, he had no idea of how able he would be to defend himself. Likewise, if Eloise was attacked, he couldn't be sure of being strong enough to protect her.

His memory flitted back to the night before, rescuing Sophie in the park above, unnecessarily as it turned out, because he could just as easily have ordered the shapeshifter to leave her alone and it would have obeyed. Unless it had attacked her for a reason.

It was unfortunate that Will couldn't converse with the creature, that it couldn't explain itself or describe what it had seen. Because Sophie had seemed innocent enough. And she had spoken words, a clairvoyant's words, that seemed to speak of a deeper connection and had even made him question his relationship with Eloise. Yet she had been to the new house, shortly before Will was himself caught in a near fatal trap there, and she had been a friend of Alex Shawcross, a boy who'd been in Wyndham's service.

Will needed to know the truth about this girl because it was potentially vital to him whichever side it fell on. If she was genuine, if the clairvoyant's words had meaning, then it remained possible that everything he'd believed these last months had been false. And if she was working for Wyndham . . . Will's thoughts floundered as he realised this was in many ways the most favourable option, not least for him and Eloise.

He was about to pick up the first of the journals when he heard the chapel door open and the sound of footsteps heading in his direction. He jumped to his feet, surprising himself even with that act, so difficult would he have found it a short while before. He picked up the swords and journals and moved silently into the ossuary.

He couldn't imagine anyone coming into the crypt this early in the day, and didn't suppose it was visited much at all. But as he stood surrounded by those walls of skulls and bones, he heard the footfall reach the top of the steps to the crypt, hesitate, then descend.

He could make out nothing for a moment, or perhaps the lightest of treads, until finally he heard Eloise say, "Will?"

He smiled, even at the sound of her voice, at the thought of her rising early to come and see him. He placed the bundle of swords in the corner, slipped the journals back into his pocket and stepped out.

Eloise smiled with what appeared to be relief, but immediately became serious as she said, "What happened? I've hardly slept." She came over and put her arms round him, holding on to him for a second before stepping back, as if determined to check that he was unharmed.

Will's thoughts tripped over her words. For one thing, she didn't look like someone who hadn't slept – she looked more rested than she'd been after the troubled sleeps she'd endured in his chambers.

"I don't understand, why didn't you sleep?"

"You're OK?" He nodded and she said, "The witches, they came to me last night. I was asleep and the window was rattling, like someone was trying to get in. Anyway, I got up and they were just hovering there, outside the window."

"Did they speak?" Even as he asked the question, he corrected himself because only one of them ever spoke.

"Not at first. I opened the window and asked if something was wrong. At first I didn't think she'd answer, but then she said . . . OK, let me get this straight . . ." Eloise paused for a second. "Yeah, she said, 'Worry not, he is safe now, but your rival has emerged and will grow in strength,' and that was it. They kind of floated away."

"You're sure it was them?"

"Of course, why wouldn't it be? But anyway, it was – I would know."

Will believed she was right about that, given Eloise's particular connection with the spirits.

"What time was this?"

She looked a little annoyed with herself as she said, "I didn't check. How stupid of me. But I'd say it was around four or five o'clock."

That made sense, and perhaps she hadn't slept much after that, but she'd slept for a good while before which explained why she looked so fresh this morning. It might have felt like a sleepless night to her, but it hadn't been. It also made sense in terms of the message the spirits had given. That would have been around the time that the shapeshifter had rescued him. The only thing that unnerved Will was the suggestion of a rival to Eloise – it could only refer to one person, and it now seemed less likely that she was Wyndham's agent and more likely that there had been something in her comment about the clairvoyant.

Eloise waited a few moments, but then said, "Well?"

"I had an eventful night, it's true. I met the spirit of a young lady up at the new house, a lady we last saw at that ghostly dinner party all those weeks ago. She sent me in the direction of her journals." He took them out of his pocket to show Eloise. "I haven't read them yet – I will do so today – but it appears she studied the labyrinth and even the writings on the walls."

"But what did they mean by you being safe now?"

He slipped the books back into his pocket and said, "As I was leaving to come back here, Wyndham had constructed some sort of electronic trap. I was slow and careless. First it blinded me, then fired a metal bolt into my heart."

Eloise's jaw dropped and she immediately put her hand on his chest, over his heart, the warmth restoring him a little further.

"What . . . but . . ."

"It's fine. As the witch told you, I'm safe now. If Wyndham had been close by, it might not have worked out so well for me. Or if I'd been left lying there past daybreak."

It pained him too, or perhaps saddened him, that the spirits of the witches had informed Eloise of his rescue, but had not intervened to help him. Indeed, he even wondered if their real reason for visiting her was solely to warn her of a potential rival.

"Can I see?" He opened his shirt and she looked visibly upset by the sight of the small puncture wound, already healing, and more so by the ghost of a scar left from the wooden stake of long ago. She traced her fingers round the older scar, then as if wanting to hide it from view, she nimbly buttoned his shirt again. "How did you get it out?"

"I think the devils we encountered in the cathedral are just the beginning of it. A shapeshifter removed the bolt for me, and there's an irony in that, because after leaving you last night I saved one of your classmates from the same creature."

The mention of the shapeshifter had placed a question on her lips, but it was superseded by the mention of a classmate.

"A classmate? Was this inside the school, or . . ."

"No, she had been to the new house. I encountered her in the park, running from the shapeshifter. I hypnotised her. She'll remember meeting me, but it's unlikely she'll talk of it or remember the details of what happened."

"She'd been to the new house? You don't think she's working for Wyndham?"

Though Will couldn't help having some suspicion, the

answer was no, the witch's words opening his eyes to what should have been obvious all along. He thought of how terrified Sophie had been, and the way she'd reacted to him, a natural fear rather than that of someone who knew who he was, who knew to avoid his gaze.

"I think not, but I do wonder if she has some other part to play – she used words that . . ."

"Who is this girl?"

"I know only that her name is Sophie – Sophia – that she's fair and from Heston . . ."

"Sophie Hamilton?" Eloise looked staggered. "You've got to be kidding me! *She's* my rival?"

Will laughed and said, "The witches may use any words they please, but I see no rival. My fate lies with you, Eloise, and only you."

As if not even hearing his final words, she said, "You don't see her as a rival now maybe, but the witches said she'll get stronger. And I've been part of this since the beginning and now . . . Sophie Hamilton! Why on earth would you be interested in her? Or did you find her *terribly, terribly attractive*?"

Will laughed again because the final three words had been delivered in a convincing impression of Sophie's voice. Thankfully, Eloise laughed at herself too.

"I am not interested in her. But tell me, presumably you believe her a bad person."

Eloise sighed, frustrated, and said, "No, she isn't. If anything, she's a bit of a goody-two-shoes. In fact, it's really not like her to be out at that time of night, and . . ." She stopped and pointed at Will, as if all the pieces had fallen together and the only explanation she needed to give was, "She was mad about Alex Shawcross."

"I know. She told me, and the night he disappeared he made some comment to her about the new house. Last night she went looking for him."

"And found you. How *terribly* lucky for both of you." Eloise was more confident now, teasing him a little. She looked at her watch. "I have to go."

He said, "Don't be obvious, but observe her today, note if her behaviour is strange, if she talks in any way about last night. If she is connected to us in some way, good or ill, we need to find out how and why."

She nodded and said with determination and defiance, "I'm the girl, the girl from the prophecies. I know it."

"So do I," said Will, smiling, and watched as she turned and walked away.

He lowered himself to the floor, leaning against one of the tombs, and took out the journals again. He would sit out here until the school came in for the morning service and then he'd retreat to the ossuary.

For a little while, he mulled over his conversation

with Eloise, and also thought of the witches appearing to her. They'd told Will they would return only once more, and he wondered if that had been the promised visit, or if they'd meant they would return to *him* only once more. He suspected they would return to Eloise as often as they felt necessary.

He opened the first of Harriet Heston-Dangrave's journals at random, and found some of the pages on which she'd tried to translate the runic writing from the labyrinth walls. He turned the pages, looking at some of her efforts, not all of them making sense.

Then, as if to reinforce that point, he saw where she'd written in a heavy and frustrated hand, "Does not make sense!" He laughed to himself, not least because that angrily written note reminded him of the lively woman they'd seen at the dinner party, not the forlorn spirit he'd encountered the night before. But as his eyes drifted across the page, he saw the small translated phrase to which this note referred and he felt a chill settle on him. It did not make sense, that was true, and that was the only aspect of it from which he could take comfort.

He will choose his queen, and his choice will be Destruction or Death.

12

They could not stand to be in the light. It was their only curse. At least, it was their only physical curse, though I'm sure there were others. I know too well what I have lost, the regrets I have, things said and not said that can never be undone. But I cannot make this about me. I have a story to tell, and would rather tell it than be forced to dwell on my own.

These four men were the first. They had gone into that cavern as kings and emerged as gods. They had developed superhuman powers, each possessing the strength of ten strong men, each able to cast others in their thrall. They did not eat or drink, yet they required, once in every season, a blood sacrifice. Their peoples offered up victims quite willingly, most often a prisoner or slave, for to have such a strong and powerful king in such tumultuous times was of no little consequence.

Did the kings understand their need for this nourishment? One did. They did not consume the blood itself so much as the life force, the very energy of the victim they fed from. That life force sustained them, and a hundred years would pass before any understood that a stake through the heart would disturb the flow of energy and render them helpless.

Nor did any but one understand the importance of the children they sired, for yes, they all kept their queens and outlived them and kept more. Those carrying the bloodline were less successful themselves in producing heirs, ensuring they would never outnumber the wider population, but they had the dual protection of offering no sustenance to the vampire kings and the promise of unending lives for themselves if they were bitten.

At least, they were promised unending lives of a sort because the creatures that returned from death did not travel all the way back to life. They could not produce children themselves and were robbed of all their human qualities. It was no wonder they considered themselves undead. They did not have what the four had shared before them.

Sivard had been a wise and good king before his encounter with the Grykken and, for the most part, so he remained after. For a hundred years he ruled over his people, in constant view during the long winter darkness, almost unseen in the lit summers.

When enemy armies determined on attacking his lands, these endless days were the times they chose, but

Sivard proved victorious time after time. Until at last, his story came to an end. In the thick of battle, by chance, a spear pierced his side and entered his heart.

Sivard fell to the floor, immediately prone, and his enemies seized their moment before his own thanes could save him. One sliced at his neck and before the entire opposing armies, Sivard vanished in a dazzling blue light.

It is said the other three kings each felt a body blow that night, long before they heard the news in their far-flung lands. And it was to presage their own fates, for no man can live forever, even those who have walked through death and returned.

Archelaos descended into depravity, but it was the love of a woman that killed him. He had lived for over two hundred years with a succession of mortal queens. The last of those queens, feeling that age was beginning to claim her, decided she could not bear to be replaced. Concealing a knife in their bedchamber, she removed his head and threw herself to her death in remorse.

Xiang Xi also survived unhindered for over two hundred years. Though the world around his eastern kingdom was beset with troubles, he maintained peace and prosperity for his people. A scholar, he had often pondered why he had not slept at all in that time, and reasoned that when he did, it would be for many years.

The time came when sleep claimed him, but Xiang Xi had planned in advance, building a royal bedchamber beneath his palace, preparing his people with promises of a golden sleeping time when he would not be seen.

The poets had done their best, but after two years, the people had grown restive. The country was threatened, and in the third year of his hibernation, barbarians sacked the royal city. Finding what they believed to be the corpse of the vampire king, they decapitated it and were left with nothing for their trouble.

The four kings had won the promise of immortality in a fight to the death with the Grykken. They had lived the spans of many lives in that time, and had left an inheritance in the bloodline of many children. Yet within less than three centuries, only one of the four survived, the one who had demanded his blood wound, the one who had stared into the Grykken's eyes and known it, Lorcan Labraid.

He had returned with his lords and followers into those haunted lands in the west, his witch muttering prophecies all the while. Labraid heeded her well, knowing the wisdom she had spoken before the battle with the Grykken. Indeed, he became jealous of her knowledge and would let her speak to no other. Labraid knew too well that the witch's words were power when spoken to him, but would be his weakness if spoken to others.

And Labraid was greedy for more. It was Sivard's death that stirred this within him. Labraid felt the body blow as the others did, but in the weeks and months following he also noticed his power increasing, as if he and the other kings had received some of Sivard's legacy upon his death.

It was as if they remained as bound together as the Grykken's four heads had been by its body. So too, Labraid's powers increased with the death of the other two, but in seeing how his power could grow, he studied the dark arts and learned from his witches, increasing his stock all the more. He even learned how to avoid the hibernation that had destroyed Xiang Xi's rule.

Could it be said that all of this was used for the benefit of his peoples? Perhaps, and perhaps not. Labraid had been a ruthless ruler even before his encounter with the Grykken, but he was touched with wickedness now. The wealth of his kingdom still proved a tempting prize to enemy invaders, and Labraid was monstrous and cruel in destroying all who came, and in expanding his own dominion over neighbouring lands.

He was spoken of with fear, and it is as well that the mists have obscured the history of that time. Labraid's *taste for spilling blood far exceeded his own need for it, and his was a dark reign.*

The key to Labraid's fate, though, lay with the witches upon whom he relied more and more. The first witch grew old and died, but just before her death, her daughter arrived at court, already a woman in middle age herself, possessed of the same gifts. So too, when she died, her daughter came, and so on over many generations.

Hundreds of years later, his witch of that time, herself nearing the end of her life, warned Labraid that his rule would be suspended. His line would triumph again, but he would have to wait many ages for the one who would come to replace him. Who was this heir, Labraid wanted to know.

She told him of this new king, a boy who would stand alone with the four royal bloodlines within him. And in finally killing Labraid, as was his duty, they would be made one, just as the four kings had been made one with the Grykken. The circle would be broken, and made whole again.

Where would this be, asked Labraid, and she told him the name of that magical place, the place that would one day be known as Marland. It would become the seat of his power, then site of his destruction, and at last the place where he would be reborn.

Could this fate be avoided, asked Labraid. No, said the witch, and what was more, it was to be embraced, for he had created it and set it in motion. He had heeded Sivard's call, stared into the Grykken's soul, been swallowed by darkness. This was his creation. Marland.

13

Will was struck most of all, as he read the journals, by the fact that his family's part in this ancient and evil history had continued to obsess some of its members long after Will's time. There had been Henry of course, who'd built this old house and the cathedral library, and the maze that was itself a map of the labyrinth. There had probably been many more besides, for it was a secret history that seemed to be passed down, but kept very much within the family, even if not all of them had understood anything of its significance.

And then there was Harriet Heston-Dangrave herself, who had apparently made it her life's work. What an extraordinary life it had been too. Not only had she explored the labyrinth many times and sought to understand it and decipher the meanings of its paintings and writings, she had also travelled and studied with the aim of fitting their family history into a much wider story. That in particular had been the reason for the many journeys to Scandinavia. Perhaps it had been inspired by the runic writing alone, but she had been convinced that the origins of this story lay in the north. Will couldn't help but agree with her when he thought of Asmund, the Viking, and of Edgar and Elfleda, Anglo-Saxons both.

She'd understood too that there were other elements to this. She'd travelled to the eastern parts of Europe and into the Near East, as far as most women would have travelled in the middle of the nineteenth century. She had also travelled to Ireland. There were several pages on what she called *The Celtic Connection* and there she mentioned Lorcan Labraid, though she did not seem to understand his significance. Even so, she had attempted to translate his name into English, settling for, *Fiercely he speaks.*

She had also guessed that Will was part of the story. He was not mentioned by name, which was all the better for Will, but at one point she had written, *Could it be that my distant ancestor's elder brother was a revenant? Though I dislike to use the hysterical terminology, could it be that this is a history of vampyres?*

The most common emotion visible in the journals, though, was that of frustration. Harriet had discovered so much, but had been constantly hindered by how much more she didn't know. Equally, she had been frustrated by the lack of material left for her by those who'd investigated the history before.

Very near the end of the second journal, her writing still strong and vibrant, suggesting she'd still been young when it was written, Will found a tantalising note – *I think I have deduced the location of the second gate, in general if not yet in the specifics. However! My progress might have been so much the quicker if Henry had left a record of his endeavours, for it is clear to me now that he knew this and more.*

Will had no doubt that he would find a great deal more of use in these journals, but he also knew that he had found them too late and that time was short. He had to hope only that the spirit of Harriet would appear to him again, because what he really needed to know was whether she'd found that second gateway, the one Edgar had probably spoken of.

The chapel was busy through the later afternoon and early evening and so Will remained in the ossuary, sitting against the door, looking up at the now familiar skull that always seemed to meet his eye. He stayed there even after silence descended beyond the door, and stood only when he heard footsteps.

He opened the door as Eloise came down the steps and she stopped as she saw him standing there and said, "How did you know it was me?"

"I noticed this morning that you skip down the first couple of steps in a very particular way."

"Do I?" He nodded and she approached and said, "How do you feel?"

He'd been so engrossed in his reading that it hadn't occurred to him, and he said, "Much better. In fact, I think my strength is back to what it was."

"Thank goodness." She pointed at the journal in his hand. "Well?"

"Very interesting, and you'll have to read them in due course." Even as he spoke, he realised that he did not want her to read the journal that spoke of two queens and a choice between destruction and death.

"But you have plans for tonight?"

"I do. Harriet speaks of being close to finding the second gateway, so I want to ascertain if she did."

"Cool. How?"

"By asking her," said Will, the answer obvious to him.

"Of course, how silly of me. For a moment I was forgetting we're in the weird world of Will and Eloise."

He laughed and said, "Eloise, I've been undead for nearly eight centuries, and until six months ago even I would have considered it strange that we now think nothing of talking to the dead."

"Well, let's hope the dead want to talk to us." She looked at the ossuary door behind him and added, "Do you still have your swords?"

"Yes, of course."

105

"Then I would bring one. Just in case the dead aren't the only people we meet."

Will nodded. "Would you like one for yourself?"

Eloise laughed at the idea. "I've told you before, I'm not wielding a sword – I really would be more dangerous to you than to anyone attacking us."

"As you wish."

He put the journal into his pocket, then stepped into the ossuary and took one of the swords from the bundle, the same one he'd used to attack the shapeshifter. He closed the door behind him and they walked in silence up from the crypt and out of the chapel.

Avoiding the kitchens, which were still full of noise, they passed by the offices and out of the door at the back of the school. Will stepped out ahead of her, but just as Eloise was about to follow him a voice sounded from within.

"Eloise? Where are you going, and at this time?"

Will recognised the voice immediately as that of Dr Higson, the headmaster.

Eloise answered, sounding surprisingly affable as she said, "Oh, hello, Dr Higson. I just needed some air."

"That's all very well, Eloise . . ."

He stopped abruptly because Will had turned and stepped back inside the doorway. He stood behind Eloise now and stared directly at Higson. The headmaster's hand was still bandaged, albeit more lightly than before, and Will noticed that he appeared to be growing something of a beard, an odd sight given his cropped hair.

Higson looked at the floor, the walls, anywhere but at Will, and his mouth moved through several soundless fragments of words before he said, "But yes, don't . . . yes, don't let anyone else . . . see you . . . leaving, that is. Carry on." He turned and walked away.

Eloise continued to stare after him in consternation, then turned and saw Will standing behind her. She was incredulous. "Did you hypnotise him?"

Will shook his head. "Let's go – I'll tell you about it."

They left quickly, before they could be disturbed again, and cut into whatever shadows were available to them with the moon so fat and bright in the sky above. Will noticed the lit windows of the Heston House common room as they walked, but very few people were in there and he couldn't see if Sophie was one of them.

As they moved away from the school, out into the park and up towards the new house, Will headed off the inevitable question by saying, "When you were . . . unwell, it was I who spoke to Higson. I'd intended to hypnotise him, but he avoided my gaze from the outset and I understood immediately. He's working for Wyndham, but I showed him a little of what I can do and his fear of me is a useful weapon in our armoury."

Eloise walked for a few paces in silence, taking in this new information, then said, "So that's why everyone's so relaxed about my absences!" She looked at Will. "Was it you who broke his hand?"

"Yes, and I could quite easily have killed him." She looked a little surprised, and he said, "You must remember, I thought I'd lost you and did not know if you would return to me. When I realised that he'd conspired with Wyndham in the attacks against you, I was overtaken with fury."

Eloise took his hand and kissed it, then didn't let it go, so the warmth of her flesh radiated through him as they crossed the park.

"All the same, I'm glad you didn't kill him."

"And the hand?"

She laughed and said, "Yes, I'll allow you the hand – serves him right."

When they rounded the stand of trees, Will cut in close rather than heading up across the lawns. He let go of her hand then and said, "I need to check that Wyndham hasn't repaired his trap."

Eloise followed him in among the trees, though he suspected that even in the moonlight she probably couldn't see anything. Will reached the tree that the shapeshifter had first pointed out to him, but the torn cables had not been repaired. He should have expected as much, given Wyndham's tendency to always move on to a new form of attack, never settling into a pattern Will could predict.

They still skirted the edge of the lawns as they made their way to the house and Will remained vigilant as he worked the lock. He opened the door, but as they stepped inside, he held Eloise by the arm and took in the air.

She whispered, "What is it?"

"I couldn't be sure . . ."

"You think there's someone in the house?" She was still whispering, but urgent now.

Will took in the air again and said, "No. It's strange, but if I was to guess, I'd say I can smell a body."

"Oh, that's all we need."

He smiled, bemused by her response in some way, and walked forward carefully towards the library. The smell was stronger there, but he was less certain now that they were about to find a corpse. It was as if a corpse had been moved through here and Will could still detect the traces of scent left behind.

They stepped into the library and almost immediately a light appeared on a table. Will braced himself, ready for an attack, but this was a gentler light than he'd encountered out on the lawns, more contained.

Even as his eyes smarted against it, Will could see that it was the screen of a laptop computer, similar to the one Rachel and Chris used.

Eloise saw it and said, "You're sure there's no one here?"

"We're alone. And there is no body, but a body was here recently."

They moved together towards the laptop, but it was Eloise who glanced around the room now and said, "We should move it to another table. It could be a trap, a device set up like outside, to hit you as you're standing there."

She picked it up and took it across the room, and all the while Will stole glances at the painfully bright but blank screen. Eloise placed it on another table and though the screen remained blank, a voice emerged from the machine, quite distinct and immediately recognisable.

"Oh, aren't you a clever one? But there is no trap here – I merely wish to talk."

Will said, "Show yourself, Wyndham, if you would talk with me."

"As you wish."

The screen flickered and Wyndham's head and shoulders appeared upon it, looking as composed and relaxed as he had in the image they'd seen three weeks ago. There appeared to be something bordering on respect too, as with the mutual respect of opposing generals, but the look in his eyes was unmistakable – for all his desire to talk, this man would not stop until Will was destroyed.

14

"Of course, we very nearly had nothing to discuss, only the manner in which I was to remove your head."

"But as you see," said Will, "I am still very much attached to it."

"It's of no matter – I always allowed for the possibility of the girl rescuing you before I could get there." Wyndham looked at Eloise. "Yet another act of folly you'll come to regret, young lady."

Eloise didn't respond, perhaps seeing as Will had that Wyndham didn't know about the shapeshifter. Will was about to ask Wyndham the purpose of this conversation when he finally made sense of what he could smell in the air around him – Alex Shawcross.

"You moved the boy's body!"

"Yes, I did."

Eloise looked at Will and said, "Alex's body?"

Will nodded, but kept his eyes on Wyndham as he said, "Have you no shame at all?"

"No shame!" Wyndham produced an outraged laugh. "For wanting his family to know that he's dead? For wanting to ensure he's given a proper burial?"

"And will you tell them that he died doing your work?"

"No, and nor will I tell them that he was murdered by a parasite."

Eloise put her hand on his arm and said, "Don't listen, Will, if he has nothing to say . . ."

"Oh, I have much to say," said Wyndham. "Don't be deceived by the failure of my little trap. While you have been idling in each other's arms for three weeks, I have been busy."

Will and Eloise glanced at each other, wondering if Wyndham had just confirmed what they'd increasingly believed themselves, that Chris and Rachel, or one of them, had betrayed them. More importantly, as Will had feared, Wyndham had no doubt used this time to rebuild his strength.

"Then speak, for we too are busy."

Wyndham nodded, and appeared more earnest as he said, "Very well. William of Mercia, I have made no secret of my desire to destroy you and your kind. You were born of evil, through no fault of your own, but you carry evil within you nevertheless. I believe even you know this and I believe you wish to do good, to do what

113

is right – yet still you do not accept the truth of it, that good will come only from your own destruction."

Will thought of the translated phrase in Harriet's journal, about his choice being one of death or destruction.

Eloise interrupted. "That isn't true! And we know it isn't true. This can end well. It will end well."

Wyndham smiled a little disarmingly as he said, "I'm sure you wish it, but you don't know what is to come."

"Nor do you – if you did, you'd tell us, but you don't."

Wyndham laughed, finally finding something admirable in Eloise's feistiness. "It is true that I don't know all of what's to come, but the more I learn the more determined I am on the only course of action."

Will was surprised at the coldness of his own voice as he said, "You have still not told us what it is that you wish to discuss."

"True," said Wyndham. "I have tried to end this at each step of the way before it escalated. Until now it has been a limited battle between good and evil, between me and you, but beyond this point, other people will be dragged in, innocents will die, and that is in the best-case scenario of my victory."

Did Wyndham glance at Eloise as he said that? Could he even see them? Will wasn't sure, but he'd sensed something in that fleeting glance, a warning for

Will alone, that Eloise would be one of those innocent victims. It brought another meaning to Harriet's advice to beware his heart because where Eloise was concerned, it *was* his weakness and he would die happily to spare her.

Wyndham continued. "Should I be defeated, the world as we know it will be turned on its head and evil will flourish. So it is that I give you one more chance to do what is right, to surrender yourself to me, to allow me to end your eight hundred years of torment."

"The answer is no." It was Eloise who'd spoken and Will turned to her now and smiled, warmed by her conviction. She looked stronger than he'd ever seen her, and turned back to the screen and Wyndham's unruffled expression as she said, "If you knew him as I know him, you'd understand that he's bigger and better than all of this, and he hasn't waited for over seven centuries to give up now. There's some goodness in all of this, there has to be, and if anyone can find it, then it's Will."

Wyndham looked unimpressed and turned slowly towards Will and said, "Her loyalty is touching, but you know best the patience of evil."

"You have heard our answer, Mr Wyndham."

"Very well, but the blood of those who die will be on your hands, not mine. And I will prevail." He looked as if he was going to say something else, his face relaxing, but he visibly cast it away and sounded hardened again as he said, "Prepare yourself, William of Mercia, the full moon is close at hand."

Wyndham's face froze and a moment later the screen died, leaving only an afterglow as the room descended back into darkness.

"Thank you," Will said to Eloise.

She turned to him, though he could tell she couldn't see him in the dark, and said, "For what?"

"For what you always do, believing in me. And for being more eloquent in my defence than I could ever be."

She smiled and shook her head, dismissive, but grew serious as she said, "What happens on the full moon?"

The full moon – Will wondered if Wyndham's warning was itself a sign of his weakness, an attempt to rattle Will with an empty threat. At the same time, he suspected a weakened Wyndham was probably more volatile and more dangerous as a result, as the bolt through the heart had so nearly proven.

"I don't know what it means, but I think it all the more important that we do what we came here for. Take my hand." Eloise reached out blindly and he escorted her out of the darkened library.

As they started up the main stairs, she said, "Where are we going? I thought we saw her in the dining room."

"We did, but I encountered her spirit last in her own room."

"OK." Eloise sounded nervous now and he couldn't quite understand why, certainly not in the light of the things she'd seen and experienced with total composure.

They reached Harriet's room and Will opened the door and stepped inside. It was moon-bathed as it had been before, and also empty. Eloise closed the door behind her and crossed the room to the window, just as Will had done. She turned to him, her figure silhouetted in the moonlit frame.

"We saw her, didn't we, or her shadow, in this window? Remember, when we were out on the lawn . . ." She stopped, probably remembering that they'd stood there with Marcus.

"I remember."

Will walked across the room to the dressing-room door and looked inside. It was empty, nor could he get the sense of her presence, or of any presence, in the room itself. Briefly he wondered if it had been a mistake to bring Eloise with him. The doubt left him, though, as he watched her. She crossed from the window and stood in front of the bureau. It was as if Eloise was picking up on the same energy that he had felt, as if he and Eloise and Harriet were all treading the same paths within this room.

117

Eloise looked down and idly opened and closed one of the empty drawers, then looked up at her own reflection in the mirror on the wall. She turned quite suddenly, staring at Will. She laughed and said, "I got a real chill then," though her words were unnecessary because she looked shaken, her eyes wide. "Just for a second, I thought I saw someone behind you."

Will turned where he stood in the open door and looked once more into the dressing room. It was still empty. When he turned back though, Harriet was standing behind Eloise, just to the side of the bureau. Will smiled and kept his voice calm as he said, "Come here, Eloise, there's something I want you to see."

But Eloise didn't move. She tried to speak, found her voice gone, and cleared her throat again before saying, "She's behind me, I can feel it. Do you see her?"

Will nodded. Again it was odd to see Eloise so nervous, so . . . afraid, when so little had fazed her until now. But it spoke of her bravery that, even feeling that way, she braced herself and slowly turned to face Harriet who now stood directly before her.

Harriet had been standing, impassive and forlorn, with the same sadness he'd witnessed on his last visit, but she smiled as she looked at Eloise and nodded as if giving approval. Then she raised her eyes to Will as he approached.

"I found your journals and they answer many questions, but they leave me with others."

Harriet nodded but looked back to Eloise and said, "What is your name?"

"Eloise."

"I see. I see." Harriet nodded, but to herself this time, as if she'd answered a question which had long puzzled her. She raised her eyes to Will once more and said, "What is it you wish to know?"

"The first gate has been destroyed, but you spoke in your journal of a second. I need to know where it is."

"Alas, I never did find it, for all my searching."

"But you knew its approximate location."

"I did indeed, and so do you, but that was of little help to me. The gate is hidden somewhere in the confines of the chapel in the old house. Henry knew it, yet he is apparently determined to hang on to that secret even now. What a troublesome old Henry he proved to be."

"What about the creatures that have escaped from the underworld? They must know their way back." She shook her head patiently. "Then tell me this – is it beyond the gate that I will find Lorcan Labraid?"

She smiled as she said, "Fiercely he speaks. I knew not how central to this entire history was Lorcan Labraid. I believe you will find him beyond the gate, and there your destiny will present itself."

"What is my destiny?"

"What would I know of that?" She looked at Eloise, briefly transfixed, and said, "I will tell you this much. Wyndham has been through the gate, and he did not go alone. I know not their names, but Wyndham was accompanied."

"Do you know anything else about them?"

She didn't answer, but slowly raised her hand as if to stroke Eloise's hair. It passed through and fell back to Harriet's side, creating a brief flickering light and a vapour-light stream of matter. She looked at Will again then and said, "Am I to take it you have chosen?"

Will looked at Eloise, but didn't answer. Eloise looked from Harriet to Will, searching for some further explanation. For Harriet, Will's silence seemed to be answer enough.

She looked forlorn again and said, "Then it is as I said. I am not here. Can it be? Can it be that I was never here, that I am a ghost and was always so?"

"You were here," said Will. "Your name is Harriet Heston-Dangrave and I have your journals."

"For how long, sir? The full moon." She pointed to the window and as they both looked she said again, "The full moon."

When they turned back, she had disappeared.

Eloise shuddered slightly, as if Harriet had walked through her, and said, "The full moon again, and what was all that about choosing and her not being here? Actually, I didn't get any of that, even by what is now my normal standards of not getting anything."

"I think the full moon is the night after tomorrow, so I imagine that mystery at least will be solved for us. But she told us something of great interest, don't you think? Come on, let's return to the school."

Eloise followed him out, saying, "Enlighten me. I mean, don't get me wrong, she said a few interesting things, but I didn't get most of it."

"She said Wyndham had been through the second gate, which means Wyndham knows where it is."

"Oh, well, let's go back into the library, boot up his magic laptop and ask him."

Will smiled, and said, "I do not imagine Wyndham would tell us, but Harriet said he didn't go alone. She didn't know *their* names, but he did not go alone. So ask yourself, who might have gone there with him?"

Eloise stopped in the hallway before reaching the door. "You think Rachel and Chris went with him?"

For some reason, Will still could not bring himself to believe that Rachel was part of Chris's treachery. He hadn't even considered Chris as the most likely companion for Wyndham's excursion into the underworld, but it was possible. If true, it perhaps also explained why Chris had been so nervous about coming back to the school.

"I think there's someone more likely, given that the gateway is somewhere within the school chapel. To be truthful, I don't know why I have not thought of it before."

"Dr Higson! Of course." Eloise laughed, and grabbed hold of Will's face and kissed him, the slightest peck before recoiling in horror at what she'd done. "Sorry. Oh God, sorry."

It was over so quickly that Will didn't even feel any pain, except for the pain of feeling the warmth of her lips pressed fleetingly against his, knowing that it was a pleasure he could never properly experience.

He laughed. "It's fine."

"It didn't . . . hurt?"

"No, it was fleeting enough to be pain-free, which sounds a terrible thing to say to a beautiful girl. And I realise too that I have not said that enough."

"What?"

"That you're beautiful. I am unable to love you as you should be loved, but I would hate you to think that I take your company and your beauty for granted because I don't."

She shook her head. "Will, I would love nothing

more than to be able to . . . actually, no, there's no way I'll make that sound as delicate as you do. So let me put it this way, being with you is the best thing that ever happened to me, and I don't need you to say anything or do anything because I see it in your eyes every time you look at me. I've never felt as loved as I have with you."

He took her in his arms, holding her, feeling the warmth of her body radiating through his, but as he stood there he couldn't shake a persistent echoing reprise of Harriet's words, "Am I to take it you have chosen?" And he couldn't forget the nature of his choice as Harriet had deciphered it from the labyrinth walls, a choice between destruction and death. What could those words mean that would end well for either of them?

Finally he eased away from her and said, "We have a visit to make."

She nodded and they stepped out through the door and into the moonlight. As Will locked the door again behind them, Eloise said, "What will you do to him?"

"Higson? Make him talk, that's all."

"Good."

And they stood for a moment, looking out across the lawns. It was so light that Will was almost tempted to take her first to the ruined walls of the old abbey, where he had so often dreamt of walking with her, but as bright as the moon was, this was no summer day. Nor did they have time for diversions. As Wyndham and Harriet had both pointed out, the full moon was at hand.

15

They hadn't walked far across the lawns when Will spotted movement against the backdrop of the distant trees. Eloise saw it a moment later as it bounded towards them.

"Oh my God! It's a hare, completely white."

"It's the shapeshifter," said Will. "Prepare to be surprised, but it will not harm you." Even as he spoke, he realised he couldn't be sure about that, given how it had responded to Sophie.

The hare bounded towards them, then leapt into the air, flipping over and landing upright before them as the schoolboy, an astounding feat of acrobatics.

Even though she'd been forewarned, Eloise stepped back and said, "What! How did you . . ." Then, as if completely forgetting what she'd seen and been told – and like Sophie, conditioned by the sight of the familiar uniform – she said, "Who are you? I've never seen you before. What house?"

The boy smiled his oddly vacant smile, and Will

smiled too and said, "He cannot speak and he is not a pupil at the school. Who knows why he takes this form?" Now that he thought of it, Will reasoned it was perhaps better not to know.

Eloise relaxed a little, but the boy appeared fixated with her in some way. He took a couple of steps forward, and though Will sensed no threat, he prepared to strike with the sword he held casually in his left hand. But the boy dropped to one knee in front of Eloise, took her hand in his and kissed it before bowing his head. He then stood again and backed away.

Eloise looked dumbfounded for a second, but said, "Thank you."

The boy smiled back at her and waited for them to start walking. He followed behind, maintaining the form of the boy for now, never catching up, never being so bold as to walk with them, but always staying a few paces behind.

After a little while, Eloise said, "Is it OK to talk in front of him?"

"Of course. He saved me after all. And is it not clear that he considers himself our servant?"

"Clear to you maybe – I'm not used to servants, remember."

"It's some considerable time since I was used to them myself." She laughed and Will went on, "I think possibly

126

it was Wyndham who unwittingly lowered the barriers to the underworld. He passed through the gate, perhaps even encountered Lorcan Labraid himself, and in some way I suspect that is why these creatures have appeared – the devils, the shapeshifter. There could be more we don't know about and more to come."

"You don't think Wyndham could've killed Lorcan Labraid?"

"If he had, would he still be so determined to destroy me?"

"And these creatures bow the knee to you because . . . well, presumably because you'll become king of the underworld?"

Will glanced at her and said, "He bowed the knee to you too." She laughed. "What sense can we make of it, of any of it? Lorcan Labraid is the Suspended King, the evil of the world, and for countless ages they have awaited my arrival that I might . . . succeed him? Then of course, they have waited another seven hundred and some years for, I can only presume, you."

Even as he said it, the voice echoed in his thoughts, that the wait had not necessarily been for Eloise alone, that there was to be a choice of queens – destruction or death. "Everyone has spoken of me as a future king, yet listening to Wyndham tonight, it did not seem that he feared the possibility of me becoming king of the underworld. His fear is that the barrier will disappear, that the underworld and this one will mingle, and that evil will flourish, all under my kingship."

They could see the school ahead of them now, the lights less inviting when set against such a bright night.

"Frankly, that sounds ridiculous."

Will laughed, which set Eloise off again. Will had no doubt that the shapeshifter was laughing silently behind them too. What a good-humoured procession they would have appeared to a casual observer, and in truth, he did feel happy as they walked down the gently sloping parkland towards the school. For whatever lay ahead, right in that moment he felt happy.

As they skirted around towards the back of the school, they saw the lit Heston House common room and stopped a short distance away and looked in at the few people still sitting around in there.

Will said, "I cannot help but think of the many nights I waited outside the Dangrave House common room for you."

"It seems an age ago, doesn't it?"

Will smiled at her choice of words, but said, "And every night Marcus seemed to know I was there. He would always turn and stare through the window. He could only have seen his own reflection there, but . . ."

"Who knows, with Marcus." Eloise pointed as a girl

strolled into the room, a tartan skirt beneath the familiar green jumper. "There's Sophie Hamilton."

At first Will thought it was a different girl. Her hair looked fairer, her skin more glowing than he remembered, but then he supposed that was to be expected now that she was in normal light. It was certainly the same girl and he could see now that she was beautiful, perhaps enough for it to have played a part in Eloise's reaction to her.

A couple of others left at around the same time and Sophie sat down in a chair with a book. The mood in the room could be described as sombre at best. Will and Eloise remained where they were and a minute or so later someone else left the room, exchanging a few words with Sophie on the way out. Unless someone was hidden from view, she was now the only person in there.

She continued to read for a minute more, then looked around casually before putting the book down and coming to the window which Will knew to be the one with the broken lock. She looked out before opening it.

Will heard Eloise say quietly, "Oh no, she's not coming out, is she?"

She was, climbing out as gracefully as she'd regained entry the night before. She eased the window back into a closed position, but then Will and Eloise heard a noise behind them and turned.

Eloise's eyes opened wide and she stifled a shocked cry. The shapeshifter had turned into the monstrous insect, but immediately clicked again into the hare which bounded away a few strides before leaping into the air and tumbling into the owl which flew away fast towards the distant trees.

Eloise looked after it and said, "That . . . giant insect or whatever it was . . . is that what . . .?"

"I don't know," said Will. "I know nothing about it other than what it is and what we see. And I also know that it does not care for Sophie Hamilton."

"Will?" They turned back towards the school. She had called out a little too loudly, and now called again. "Will?"

"I should go to her or the whole school will join us."

He walked forward hastily. Sophie was walking out on to the lawns herself, but hesitated briefly when she saw the figure emerging out of the night.

"Will, is that you?"

"It is."

"I knew you'd be here." She approached quickly now, holding him by the shoulders, kissing him on the cheek as if they were old friends.

Will involuntarily found himself dissecting her scent, the healthy blood flowing just below the warm skin of the cheek that brushed against his. He also found

130

himself dissecting Eloise's reaction to this display of affection. As if hearing his thoughts, Sophie let go and stepped back.

"Sorry, didn't mean to invade your space." She laughed. "How terribly rude of me – we hardly know each other, but then you did save my life. Isn't that funny? It should be a shocking thing to say, but really it doesn't *feel* shocking at all."

Will was impressed by how effective his hypnosis had been. He could also hear Eloise approaching slowly behind him now, and then a moment later Sophie looked over his shoulder and did a double take.

"Eloise? Hello!"

"Hello, Sophie."

Sophie looked from Eloise to Will and then back to Eloise as she said, "Do you know Will as well?"

He caught Eloise's expression and smiled, letting her know that he found the tone of Sophie's question amusing. As if that smile had restored her shaken confidence, Eloise also smiled. "Yeah, we've known each other for a little while."

"We only met last night. Will saved me from . . ." She looked at Will, swimming up from the confusion that had flooded her thoughts, perhaps also wondering if she was allowed to tell Eloise. He nodded, and she said, "I know this sounds crazy, but did you save me from a monster . . . no, a shapeshifter, like a monster one minute and a boy . . .?"

"Yes, I did."

She smiled in satisfied amazement, still protected from the shock of it all by the remains of his hypnotic spell. So she looked incredulous but relaxed as she said to Eloise, "I suppose you're used to all this, if you've known each other a while, but isn't it all terribly exciting?"

"Yeah, but as you said, we're used to it."

Will smiled again, amused and touched by Eloise's desire to build a protective wall around her and Will, with Sophie firmly on the other side of it.

Sophie, for her part, appeared not to notice, but glanced back towards the empty common room before saying to Eloise, "This isn't official yet, but word got out this evening – they found Alex Shawcross's body this morning, at a place called Puckhurst. Apparently he killed himself."

Puckhurst! What a perverse choice, even for a taunt, which Will thought was undoubtedly the intention.

Eloise said, "Oh, I'm so sorry, Sophie, I know you really liked him."

"Thanks." She turned to Will. "That was the boy I was looking for last night."

"I remember. I'm sorry for your loss." It stung him to

offer condolences when he knew the truth of it, but then, Sophie didn't look like someone who'd lost her first great love. She almost appeared more taken up with the intrigue and drama of a fellow pupil committing suicide than she was upset at his death. With an additional pang of guilt, Will wondered if his hypnotism had also numbed her emotions to that news.

She looked back to Eloise and said, "Dr Higson left tonight to see his family, or the police, or something, and I think he'll be making an announcement in chapel, but it won't be till Monday probably, what with the exeat."

"What exeat?"

"This weekend. Oh, it must've been while you were away. Higson moved the exeat, but it's not a proper one because a few people can't leave. I'm one of them – my parents are in New York. Nearly everyone else is leaving tomorrow."

"What's an exeat?"

Sophie looked confused, surprised that Will didn't know.

Eloise sounded distracted as she explained. "It's er . . . it's a weekend when everyone leaves the school, but they're fixed, so it's really odd that Higson should change it."

Sophie said, "So are you staying too?" Eloise nodded.

"Great, well then, we'll have fun, won't we? I thought it might just be me at one point. My parents are terribly annoyed about it."

Will looked at her and said, "Did Dr Higson give a reason for changing the dates of the exeat?"

"Yes, he did. It was something to do with urgent maintenance work, but a lot of people weren't happy about it."

"So Higson has gone away." He left that comment hanging there for a moment, making sure Eloise had understood the implication.

She did and responded in kind by saying, "And the school will be almost empty tomorrow night, and the night after."

Sophie said, "So what are you doing now? Do you mind if I tag along?"

Eloise looked ready to make excuses, but Will threw her a glance, asking her to bear with him, and said, "We're going into the chapel. And you are more than welcome to join us."

"The chapel?" Sophie looked bemused. "That all sounds terribly mysterious."

Eloise looked at her in consternation and said, "Sophie, you were attacked by a shapeshifter last night and saved by a boy carrying a sword – you really think exploring a chapel's mysterious in that context?"

"No, I suppose not, if you put it like that. And he had a bundle of swords last night, didn't you, Will?"

Her tone rankled Eloise, the tone of someone suggesting she knew Will better. Will could see Eloise swallowing the irritation, resisting the desire to tell Sophie she'd been there when Will had been given that bundle of swords.

A light went out and they saw that the Heston House common room had now descended into darkness. Several other lights had gone out too, in the time they'd been standing there.

Sophie said, "We can get in through Heston – the window doesn't lock properly."

This time Eloise couldn't resist saying, "No, we use the door into the kitchens – it's closer to the chapel."

"But . . ."

"Trust me," said Eloise. "We've been doing this for some time."

They walked on, and Eloise looked at Will several times, her expression confused by his lack of caution. He knew what he was doing though, and time was too short.

If Sophie had a connection with his destiny, she could prove useful to them now, or even crucial. In the unlikely event that she was working for Wyndham, nothing would be learned by the sorcerer from the knowledge that Will was exploring the chapel. And if Sophie *was* working for Wyndham and Will was lucky, they might even learn something themselves from her behaviour.

16

Once the chapel door was closed behind them, Sophie looked at Eloise and said, "Aren't you a revelation? I knew about you running away, but . . ."

"But?"

"I just assumed you were into drugs or something. Sorry, that sounds awfully rude. I don't mean you look like the kind of person who'd be into drugs, but you know, the whole running away thing. And I don't mean I didn't think you were interesting or anything. I just didn't know you, I suppose."

"It's OK, Sophie, I understand what you're trying to say. And I have been a bit of an absent figure this year."

"Who can blame you?" Will noticed her give Eloise a conspiratorial nod of the head in his direction. Eloise winced slightly in response. Then Sophie turned to Will and said, "So what are we looking for?"

"A secret passage of some . . ."

"A-mazing! This is all terribly exciting. Where does it lead to?"

"Let's not worry about that for the time being. The fact is, somewhere in the chapel there's a hidden entrance to a passage underground and I need to find it." Sophie looked ready to speak again, her excitability understandable given her muddled thoughts and the influx of new experiences. But Will cut in quickly, saying, "It's unlikely to be in the crypt, but it could be anywhere else."

He realised he still hadn't explored the various tombs within the crypt, but he doubted now that he would find the entrance there. This chapel had been built by Henry after all, a man who'd loved puzzles, who'd built the complex library at the cathedral, so it was unlikely that he would have taken the obvious route of building the crypt round the second gateway.

Eloise said, "We should split up."

"That's what they do in films – it's never a good idea."

Eloise laughed, genuinely amused, and said, "True, but we're not exploring a creaky old house, we're exploring a chapel with which you and I are very familiar."

Sophie looked at Will and said, "She's got a point. I'll start at the other end."

She walked off and Eloise shrugged her shoulders at Will, as if to remind him that he had invited Sophie along. They also separated and Will walked up the chapel and left the sword at the top of the crypt steps, then started to work his way back down the side of the building.

In a sense it was the least likely place because this was the outside wall of the chapel, but with Henry behind the construction, anything was possible. Even so, he'd covered half the wall without finding anything remotely promising when he heard Sophie's voice, sounding as if from some distance away.

"Er, Will, Eloise?"

He made a mental note of the point he'd reached and then turned. Eloise was on the opposite side and she looked over at Will before they both headed past the altar, across from where the crypt was situated. There the chapel extended into a sort of alcove and there was a door to a vestry, but in the opposite corner, almost behind the altar, Sophie was staring at the wood panelling of the wall.

She turned to them and then pointed in front of her saying, "You might think this is a teeny bit obvious, but I've never noticed it before – this is a door. It's locked, but I'm sure you could pick it."

She had been behind Will as he'd opened the door into the school and hadn't realised that he'd used only his mind to do so. Will stood in front of the small wooden door and looked at the lock.

He turned to Sophie and said, "Just to err on the side

of caution, I wonder if you could get my sword? I left it by the steps to the crypt."

"Of course. So you think this could be it?"

"I don't know, but it's more promising than anything we've yet found."

Sophie went to get the sword and Will immediately put his hand over the lock, feeling the mechanism shifting beneath his fingers. At the same time, Eloise said, "It's a little obvious, don't you think? I mean, sure, we haven't noticed it before, but it is still a door. My guess is it's an old storeroom."

As soon as the lock was freed, the door opened into the room. The interior didn't look promising, but Will reached in and flicked the switch near the door which filled the room with a bright bare light. He wanted to put on his dark glasses but just then Sophie came back with the sword.

She held it out to him and said, "It has a lovely weight to it."

"You know about swords?"

"Yes, I fence, with a foil, but I have used a sabre. Nothing quite like this though." She looked into the room. "Hmm, not as exciting as I'd hoped."

Will's eyes had become accustomed to the light by now and he stepped inside as he said, "Too soon to tell."

They followed him inside. It was a small, empty,

rectangular room, and Eloise was almost certainly right, it probably had once been a storeroom. The walls were wood-panelled and Will made his way around them, feeling the wood, tapping it, trying to get a sense of there being an opening beyond.

With the exception of the wall with the door in it, all the rest sounded more or less hollow. Will frowned, wondering if the wooden walls had been made purposefully smaller than the stone walls within which they sat. It would be an easy way of hiding a priest-hole within plain sight, though he couldn't imagine that the Earls of Mercia had ever needed such a hiding place. It could just as easily have been a miscalculation on the part of the craftsmen who'd constructed it, but given that this chapel had been built by Henry, Will suspected there was more to this room than met the eye.

There was a wooden parquet floor and when he turned away from the walls, he noticed Eloise was on her knees across the room, inspecting the point where floor met wall. Sophie looked at him, then at Eloise, and made a comical grimace, as if they were both equally puzzled by Eloise's behaviour.

He understood exactly what she was looking at though, and as he approached she said, "I know this sounds strange, but I don't think the walls are attached to the floor. I can't be sure because it looks solid enough,

141

but it's almost as if the walls are freestanding."

Will nodded. "These three walls are all hollow. It doesn't mean anything lies beyond them, but it merits further investigation."

Sophie smiled broadly, pleased with herself, but then said, "Where do you live, Will?"

Eloise looked alarmed, but Will was relaxed as he said, "I live in the city, near the cathedral, but I'll be staying here this evening. I'm quite nocturnal."

Sophie stared at him, still smiling, and for the first time he was a little troubled by her stare because, also for the first time, he really did feel that there was a connection of some sort there. He looked at Eloise and suspected she'd noticed it too.

"This little room has potential, but we should search the rest of the chapel and then, I fear, you two will have to bid me goodnight."

Sophie turned to Eloise and said, "Does he always talk like that?"

"Most of the time. I'm working on him."

They searched on for another hour, but found nothing else that was even suggestive of a tunnel or passageway. Will thought of Harriet Heston-Dangrave carrying out the same search a century and a half before, while he was just a short distance away in the city. Harriet might have spent days or even weeks searching, and would have had the permission and resources to take the storeroom apart if she'd suspected it of harbouring a secret. Yet she had found nothing of the second gateway, which made it so much less likely that they would be successful in the brief time they had remaining.

When Eloise and Sophie left, Eloise made a point of saying, "I'll walk back with you as far as your room, Sophie."

"Oh, thanks. Goodnight, Will."

"Goodnight. Sleep well."

He merely exchanged a glance with Eloise, and neither felt the need to say anything, certainly not in front of someone else. She smiled and Will closed the chapel door as they crept away into the darkened school.

Once alone, he walked to the front of the chapel and sat in one of the pews. Even in here, the moon illuminated the interior, softened only by the stained glass of the windows. He closed his eyes and tried to empty his mind, hoping that the answer would come to him.

Several times he thought of the storeroom, but his mind returned more often to the crypt, the one place he was certain Henry would not have concealed the entrance to the second gateway. He wondered if Henry had even known the true nature of these gateways, or if he had ever passed through them as Wyndham had.

Finally he stood and went back to the storeroom, and

in darkness he moved around the walls, feeling his away across the surface of the panelling, searching out some mechanism that might open a hidden door. He found nothing and was in the process of starting his search anew when he heard the chapel door open.

It had been at least an hour since Eloise and Sophie had left, though he could quite easily imagine that Eloise had decided to come back, no doubt to discuss the sudden appearance of Sophie. He also didn't doubt that Eloise would distrust her, as instinctively as Will had always distrusted Chris.

For the moment he stayed where he was, in case this was not Eloise but a visitor with other plans. So he waited, listening to the steps progress softly up the chapel, almost inaudible even to him, then grow fainter still again. She was heading to the crypt.

Will left the storeroom and stepped back out into the chapel. He could see a light emerging from the crypt steps, candlelight rather than a torch. He followed, but by the time he reached the top of the steps, the light had moved into the first room of the crypt itself.

He was halfway down the steps when he heard her say, "Will?" Her voice was nervous, uncertain. He turned at the bottom and saw Sophie there, looking through the second room towards the ossuary door.

"I'm here."

She turned, guarding the flame with a cupped hand, and sighed as she said, "That's a relief. Where were you?" She was wearing a nightshirt and bedsocks, and managed to look no less attractive for it.

"I was in the storeroom."

"Oh, I didn't see a light or I would've gone there."

"What are you doing here, Sophie?"

"Are you annoyed?"

"Not at all, just curious."

She smiled, her face aglow in the candlelight, and said, "Me too." He didn't respond and a second later, she said, "I didn't really believe you'd be staying down here all night. I mean, seriously, who are you, Will? You look around our age, so what are you doing walking around in the countryside in the middle of the night, carrying swords, fighting monsters, saving damsels in distress. It's just crazy. And why are you spending all night in a chapel looking for some terribly secret passage?"

"Do you mind if I ask you a question first?" Sophie shrugged, the flame dancing for a moment before settling again. "You just came into a darkened chapel, so the most likely conclusion would have been that I'd misled you, that I wasn't here. Yet you walked directly through the chapel and down into the crypt. Why?"

"You left your sword at the top of the crypt steps earlier. It's not like you could sleep anywhere else in the chapel, not without the risk of being found in the morning. So I guessed you must be sleeping in the crypt. I have to admit, just before you showed up, I was beginning to get a bit nervous. I mean, seriously, how can you sleep down here?"

He walked slowly towards her and said, "Why don't you put the candle on the tomb there."

She looked to her left and placed the candle on the flat tomb. When she turned back, Will was directly in front of her. She was a little shorter than Eloise, but looked up into his eyes now, which once again suggested she was nobody's spy. And those eyes were full of excitement and nervousness.

"You want to know who I am?"

She gave a faint nod, then said, "But Will, I don't want you to think I'm the sort of girl who . . ."

He put his hands on her shoulders, feeling the warmth of her skin through the material of the nightshirt, and he stared back into her eyes. He was about to tell her that he was not that kind of boy either, but from nowhere, he found other words on his tongue and said, "Sophie, I am in love with Eloise, and have been for a long time, perhaps as long as I can remember."

He lowered his hands again and she smiled, embarrassed, as she said, "Of course you are. Eloise is beautiful, and probably the most confident, self-assured person I've ever met." She laughed as she said, "It's sickening."

Will laughed too, but said, "You're beautiful too, and in another time, who knows?" She nodded, but even as she did, he intensified his stare, hooking her into his world again, and said, "Why were you at the new house, Sophie?"

Her voice came back as if she was talking in her sleep, "Alex. I was looking for Alex."

"Did you like Alex?"

"I think so. I'm not sure now. I met Will . . . You're Will. I've known you a long time, I think."

Her words were so surprising that he almost lost his concentration, almost let her go again. But one such comment on its own meant nothing.

"Who is Wyndham?"

She shook her head lightly in confusion as she said, "I don't know. It's a name I don't recognise."

"Did anyone ask you to find me?"

"No." Even within her trance she sounded surprised by the question, then said softly, "But you found me. You saved me."

"Do you know who I am, Sophie?"

"Will." Even as he looked into her eyes, it seemed to him that she fell away now, into some deeper place, his mind reaching down into the subconscious thoughts, and when she spoke again, her voice sounded oddly certain and composed. "You are William of Mercia, he who will be king, and I am your queen."

Again he had to brace himself against the shock of her words, but after a moment, he said, "A man cannot be a king without a kingdom. Over what will we reign?"

Her eyes opened wide, a wild driven quality about them, as if she was no longer within his trance, but drawing on ancient memories, and she sounded full of conviction as she said, "You will be a king, My Lord, and I will be your queen, and we will lay waste to all before us, and our realm will be destruction."

Will closed his eyes and a moment later he heard her say, her normal voice returned to her, "Oh God, what happened, I just . . . I didn't fall asleep?"

He opened his eyes again and smiled at her, "You were a little faint, but you're fine now."

"But, My Lord . . ." Sophie stopped, cocking her head to one side and looking staggered as she said, "Where did that come from? Sorry, Will, I meant to say . . . actually, I think I should go to bed. I'm so tired and it's been such a strange couple of days."

"I'll walk you back to the chapel door."

"Shall I bring the candle?"

"Only if you need to."

She smiled. "No, I'll leave it here for you. You'll

have to hold my hand, but I'm sure Eloise will forgive you that."

He took her hand and led her up the steps and into the chapel, and from her words he judged she had no idea of what she'd said in the trance, that it was buried deep.

At the chapel door he said, "Will you find your way from here?"

"Of course, and thank you." He was about to say that she had nothing to thank him for, when she lifted his hand to her mouth and kissed it. Instantly she said, "Just until the time comes."

"What time?"

She put her hand on her chest and said, "Seriously, I have no idea why I said that. Ignore me, I'm tired. Goodnight, Will."

Her expression suggested she was telling the truth, that she didn't know why she'd spoken or acted like that. Could anyone be so good an actor? Could anyone continue to act the innocent even through his hypnotic spell? He doubted it, but if she spoke true, the implications filled Will with greater concerns.

"Goodnight again."

Sophie walked away quickly and he closed the chapel door and strolled back down to the crypt and the candle. "Does not make sense!" Harriet had written above her translation, and he wished it still didn't. *He will choose his queen, and his choice will be Destruction or Death.*

The choice had not yet presented itself, not in any real sense, and for the time being, Will didn't believe there was any choice to be made. For as he had said to Sophie, he was in love with Eloise, a love that felt as if it had always been.

Yet from her trance, and it *had* been from within a trance, Sophie had declared herself. She was one of the queens, one of his choices, and what she offered was destruction. Which meant, in some way he couldn't understand, that Eloise represented the other choice. Eloise who had been everything that was good in his life, she was death.

17

He tapped her on the shoulder, and the material of her blouse was warm where the sun had been on it. And now he saw that the sky was blue and dotted with unthreatening white clouds. He could feel the warmth on his own skin, a warmth that also reminded him of her. Eloise turned and smiled at him.

He could hear other voices nearby, talking in a tongue he did not understand, but he could see, and wanted to see, only her.

"I waited for you," she said, and stepped towards him. "I waited."

He reached out and pulled her towards him and they kissed, a kiss so familiar, but the heat disappeared from his skin and he felt a chill, as if one of those tiny clouds had covered the sun. He pulled back a little and saw that it was Sophie he held.

She smiled, but stepped away from him and jumped up on to the crumbling remains of the abbey walls. The sky no longer looked the same blue, but rather as if something darker had stained it, and now there were no other voices. Sophie laughed and he felt the ground trembling beneath him, and he too stepped backwards up on to one of the low walls.

The ground shook, and when he looked down, the grass on which they'd been standing was falling away, a bottomless chasm opening up. He looked across the abyss to where Sophie still stood on the old stump of wall. She was wearing the nightshirt and bedsocks, and laughing as she said, "We did this, Will! This is ours!"

And he opened his eyes. For weeks Will had wanted to slip away into one of his waking visions and at last it had come, but it had left him even more adrift than the usual frustration of being shown a world he could not know. Nor could he make sense of it because he could no more associate Sophie with destruction than he could Eloise with death.

He put it out of his mind and stared ahead. He was sitting in the ossuary, facing his familiar skull. It looked as if it had moved and appeared to be staring askance at him now, almost as if it had attempted to turn away from him. Will got up from the floor and straightened the skull, finding it looser in its position than he'd imagined.

He walked out into the crypt then, just as Eloise came in at the other end.

"You're early."

"I know, it isn't even quite dark yet. But the school's virtually empty, no lessons, so I was free."

He closed the ossuary door and she walked towards him and said, "It seems it's now customary to kiss you on the cheek."

Will smiled and held her and stroked her hair, full of regret that he couldn't be even a little more human for her. "She came to see me last night."

"I know." Her voice was hot and muffled against his neck, but then she pulled away and said, "She said you told her that you're in love with me."

He nodded. "Yes, I'm sorry, I shouldn't have spoken of it to someone we know so little."

Eloise laughed, saying, "No, trust me, Will, I'm quite happy for you to tell Sophie Hamilton that you're in love with me. And it's me who should be embarrassed – I was a bit jealous, which is silly, I know."

"Not at all. She's pretty and forward and she believes she has a connection with me."

"Do you?"

"No." He felt he was lying, though he didn't believe she was to be his queen. He still didn't entirely believe that he could be a king, but that was as nothing when compared to casting Eloise in the role of death, something that was beyond his comprehension. "But I'm

153

surprised she let you come alone now. Where is she?"

Eloise smiled and said, "She is quite sweet. As she now thinks we're an item, she thought you and I would want some time alone, to make out, you know."

"How disappointed she would be."

"I think she'd be even more envious if she knew the truth." Eloise looked at her watch. "I think as soon as it gets dark we should try to get into the city, rather than have to explain to Sophie where we're going. I assume you *do* want to ask Chris about the gateway."

Will nodded. "Asking won't be enough this time. I'll have no choice but to put him in a trance, to force the truth out of him, and if he has been innocent all this time, then we'll certainly lose him as a friend after that."

"Yeah, putting it like that, I'm less convinced. Higson will be back tomorrow lunchtime if you'd rather wait."

"That wouldn't leave us a great deal of time. Tomorrow night is the full moon, and whatever is set to happen, both Wyndham and Harriet are agreed on its significance. We have to go to Chris this evening."

"Good, because I've ordered a taxi for an hour's time. It'll be dark by then." Eloise frowned then and said, "When you told her last night that you were in love with me, why did you say it? Did she hit on you?"

"Hit on what?"

She laughed loudly and said, "Oh, I do wish you'd

learn some modern slang. And by modern I probably mean anything since the English Civil War."

"There was a civil war?"

She looked briefly astounded before realising he was joking, and said, "But you really don't know what it is to hit on someone?"

He shook his head. "Presumably it refers to something amorous."

"Exactly, did she make an advance, did she throw herself at you?"

"I see. Not quite. In fact, she was at pains to point out that she isn't the kind of girl who does that sort of thing."

"Oh." Eloise looked disappointed. "Makes me look a bit cheap, doesn't it? Mind you, I'm slightly embarrassed by a lot of my behaviour when we first met. I said . . . some stupid things."

"Eloise, the only extraordinary thing about your behaviour when we met was how unruffled you were by everything. You fainted when you discovered I have no pulse, but I seem to remember the discovery of my true condition filled you with a mixture of excitement and longing rather than the horror it should have induced."

"Because I already knew I was safe. At some level, I just knew it." She smiled wistfully, but snapped out of it and said, "Did you find anything in the storeroom?"

"No, but I do have a feeling that might be the place. All the more reason to speak to Chris."

The school had the air of a deserted building by the time they went out and met the taxi at the gate. Eloise could have asked for the car to come up the drive, but had reasoned Sophie might have spotted it and asked to come along.

"Beautiful night," said the driver once they were in and headed for the city.

Eloise glanced out of the window and said, "It is, but if you don't mind, we'd prefer not to talk."

"Suit yourself," said the driver.

Will reached out and held her hand, a reminder of a previous journey when one of his visions had come to him. No vision came this time, and after the one he'd experienced earlier, he was glad of that.

It was Friday night and the city was busy and raucous, but as they headed down the narrow street towards The Whole Earth, Will could see an odd pocket of darkness ahead of them. The explanation was plain as soon as they got there – the café was closed and in darkness.

A couple were standing at the door, looking in, and they turned to Will and Eloise and the man said, "It's closed. I only called this morning to ask if I needed a reservation."

The woman shrugged. "Never mind, let's find

somewhere else – I could eat some meat anyway." They left and Will and Eloise took their place. There was no sign of light coming from even the back rooms.

"Do you want to work the lock?"

Will looked around – there were plenty of people walking about in the street. He looked at the upper floor too, but it was all in darkness. "Let's go round the back."

"OK, but I think something must be seriously wrong if they were still answering the phone this morning."

They moved round to the back of the property. The car was gone, but Will could see a small light now, and as they neared the kitchen he saw what it was. Rachel was sitting at the kitchen table, in front of her a single lit candle, a glass of wine and an open bottle.

Eloise tapped the window and Rachel looked up. Her expression was transparent, one of hope, followed by thinly veiled disappointment. She looked tired too as she got up and came to open the door.

Eloise said, "Rachel, what's wrong?"

"He's gone, left." Rachel sounded as if she'd given up on life, but her deeply ingrained manners came to the fore and she appeared to rally as she said, "I'm sorry, do sit down." As they sat across the table from where she'd been sitting, Rachel took another glass and poured some wine into it for Eloise.

"Thanks," said Eloise, though she didn't drink. Rachel sat down again and Eloise said, "Did he say where he was going?"

Rachel shook her head, but then looked at Will and said, "You've known for a long time, haven't you?"

"I've suspected, but I wanted to believe in him."

"So did I. But that's where he's gone. I don't know where exactly, but he said Wyndham needed him. You could've knocked me over, after all his denials and playing the innocent, to come out with it just like that."

Will took the final confirmation in his stride and could think only what it meant in terms of the threat posed by Wyndham.

"Did he say why Wyndham needed him?"

"Oh yes, apparently a great battle is at hand. Not that I can see how he'll be any use there." She sipped from her wine glass, but Will realised she wasn't drowning her sorrows and was actually quite sober. "He wanted to assure me too that you're nothing less than evil. He kept banging on about how you'd tried to bargain our blood for Eloise's at Puckhurst."

"That's ridiculous!" Eloise was more offended by the suggestion than Will was himself. "Will was just trying to get Asmund to let me go. You know that. You know he wouldn't have let him kill you."

"I know that, but Chris was adamant."

Will tried to think back to that night, with Chris and Rachel caught in Asmund's trance, Eloise in his grip. It was true Will's only thought was to free Eloise, but would he have fought as hard to save Chris and Rachel?

If that was the reason for the treachery, he even admired Chris to some extent, because in his mind he was repaying a greater treachery on Will's part. He had still cast himself as Will's enemy though, and Will would treat him as such from now on.

Expressing something he'd sensed for some time, perhaps from the start without realising it, Will looked at Rachel and said, "For what it's worth, Asmund might well have fed on Chris, but you would have provided no nourishment for him." She looked at him questioningly, as if wanting to be clear on what he was saying. "You carry the line."

"Oh." She looked at Eloise and said, "What a strange thing to discover."

Eloise in turn looked at Will as she said, "Is there any way back for him, afterwards? I mean . . ."

"No," said Will.

"But . . ."

"Eloise, Will's right. He's betrayed all of us, and me most of all. There's no way back from that."

Will looked at Rachel. "You must rue the day you

filmed me, and even more the day you met me."

She shook her head, not so much in disagreement as despair. "What's the point? It happened. And more and more I think nothing happens by chance."

"Perhaps you're right."

Even so, Will couldn't help but think of the many people who'd had good reason to rue the day they'd met him – good Kate, Arabella, Rachel and Chris, his many victims. It was possible yet that Eloise would come to regret it most of all.

Will stood, and both Rachel and Eloise looked at him in surprise, but he said, "I'm sorry to leave you when you need us most, but if there is a battle, it will be tomorrow and there's still so much for me to do."

"I understand." Rachel reached a hand across the table to Eloise and said, "Take care. Especially now."

"I will," said Eloise. "Thanks for the wine." She hadn't touched it, but she too stood and they walked through the city and found a taxi to take them back to the school gates.

They hardly spoke on the return journey, because nothing needed to be said. They both understood that Chris's disappearance had set back their plans to find the second gateway. And they both realised that one mystery at least had finally been explained – Chris *had* betrayed them, and they also knew why.

The taxi left them at the gate and they walked up the drive. Once they'd cleared the trees it was a surprise to see the school so much in darkness. From the front they could count only three lights.

Will noticed movement on the lawns to his right and looked across to see the shapeshifter in the form of the boy. He stood, looking at them, but did not move further or attempt to approach – Will wondered if the creature was being cautious after last seeing them with Sophie, though he still couldn't understand its aversion to the girl.

He said quietly, "Our friend the shapeshifter is across to our right."

"You mean left."

"No, he's . . ." Will turned and spotted the boy to the left of the drive. He looked back to the right, but not only was the boy still there, Will could also see another identical figure off across the lawns.

Eloise saw them too. "OK, now *that's* pretty weird."

Another stood on the lawns near the school, and Will looked behind and saw three more. It was as if they were dotted across the entire parkland, standing passively, all in the form of the boy.

Eloise stopped walking and looked around. Will stopped too, and then the boys all moved at once, jumping up into the air with remarkable agility, then

161

changing into something resembling a black serpent before disappearing into the ground.

The parkland was empty once more and after a moment Eloise said, "Did you notice, they were completely synchronised?"

"As if they're all part of the same creature."

They started to walk again and she said, "Kind of creepy, don't you think, seeing them all standing there? Creepy in a good way of course."

Will laughed. "How so?"

"They're on our side."

"True."

They had almost reached the main doors when they noticed more movement, like birds on the roof, disturbed by their approach and taking off into the night. But these were much bigger than birds, and as they took flight against the illuminated night sky, it was immediately apparent that two of the devils they'd encountered in the cathedral had been perched up on the roof of the school.

"More of our allies," said Will, though he immediately saw the significance of it.

Eloise stopped and looked at him. "It's like they're gathering, ahead of tomorrow, like they all know what's coming."

"A battle," said Will. "Remember the vision I told

you about, of a great battle taking place here in ancient times? The only thing that puzzles me – I see our allies, and I am grateful that we have any, but where is the opposing army?"

"I have a feeling it won't just be Wyndham and Chris." Eloise smiled. "But look on the bright side, we could get to the gateway first."

Will smiled too because they had no idea what they would encounter on the other side of it. All he knew for certain was that this battle was Wyndham's business, and it only had one aim: to prevent him from passing through that gate.

18

arland! It was a place I knew so little in life, and yet it speaks to me now as deeply as if I had known it always. And that place sums up in my own mind everything that . . . No, I've determined once already that I won't dwell on my own sadness here. And nor should I – for am I not blessed? I am here only to play the bard, until my own time comes, and that is what I shall do.

But it was to the place we now know as Marland that Lorcan Labraid moved his court, and it was from there that he ruled. After living with many mortal queens, he tired of losing his companions to age and took a queen who carried the line, a distant descendant of Sivard. Her name was Elfleda, but their reign together lasted only one more lifetime, the lifetime of another witch.

That witch was the daughter of the one who had prophesied his fall and rise again, but when she died, no replacement came. One year elapsed, then another, but the rhythm which had been Labraid's only constant these centuries past seemed ground to a halt.

Then at last a young maiden appeared, the grand-daughter of the previous witch, a girl whose own mother had died two years before. Labraid welcomed her, but Elfleda grew jealous of the girl's beauty and apparent sway over her king.

Little by little, Elfleda poisoned Labraid's mind against the girl. The young witch, sensing the cruel fate that awaited her if she remained, escaped by morning light, journeying south to the kingdom of those who still controlled their own destinies.

She was welcomed by the nobles of that southern kingdom, and when she saw from afar the nature of Labraid's evil reign, she set about telling her hosts how they might defeat the great immortal ruler. The future was hers to see, as it had been for generations of the women before her, and she warned her hosts that they could not expect to kill Labraid, but only imprison him.

So it was that a vast army marched on Labraid's stronghold. For his part, Labraid was not surprised when the messenger warned of the approaching warriors. He had long expected it, and already knew the likely outcome. Labraid had lived long enough to be able to see beyond the day ahead.

Bidding farewell to his queen, he gave her assurances and instructed her on how to prepare for the times to come. He told her not to seek him again, but to await the one who would follow him. This is how it came to pass that it was Elfleda who escaped and Lorcan Labraid who stayed to await his fate.

Labraid and his army met the enemy on open ground at Marland. It was a full moon, as befitted the witch's request. The southern army glistened in the moonlight, its armour and weaponry polished so much that it looked like a silvern sea sparkling there.

Labraid's warriors were battle-hardened, but when combat commenced they suffered many losses, outnumbered and outmanoeuvred by their skilled and determined enemies. Only the presence of Labraid himself, in the middle of the battlefield, maintained their spirits.

Lorcan Labraid cut down all who came close, but the witch had warned the army of her hosts to avoid him in the first part of the battle. So it was that Labraid rushed around the meadow in a fury, slicing down men whenever he could reach them, becoming more and more frustrated that so few came within reach. He was in too much of a rage to see how depleted his own ranks were becoming.

The moon was low in the sky now, behind Labraid's army. And then, at the witch's command, her new champions angled their polished shields to reflect the moon's beams at Labraid. It only served to drive him into an ever greater frenzy, but blinded, he was weakened.

A brave detachment charged towards him. Even with Labraid disabled, five lost their lives before he was subdued. The metal plate he wore across his chest was torn away from him and the young witch herself drove a stake through the fallen king's heart.

Immediately one of the warriors sought to remove his head, ignoring the warnings the witch had given. Labraid's dark powers were still strong, though his body was weakened, and the sword struck his neck as a plough strikes a rock in the ground. Instantly the man's blood left his body as a vapour, which was taken by the laughing Labraid. And then his erstwhile attacker crumbled to dust before their very eyes.

"Heed my words," cried the witch. And though some of the warriors had doubted her, the sight of their friend leaving not even a body to honour was enough to bring them to silence now. "His magic will ensure that only one can kill him, but my magic will ensure that none can save him."

Labraid laughed, even in his imprisonment, and said, "Witch, you did well to leave my service, for you have done my service better than you ever could at my side. It is as the prophecy said, and I will bide my time."

167

The witch turned to the warriors and said, "Go tell your king a barrow will be built here, a construction I will oversee, and they must do as I wish in exchange for the kingdoms I have given them."

The warriors departed and the witch was left alone in the middle of the moonlit meadow surrounded in every direction by the dead of that great battle.

"Lorcan Labraid, my great-grandmother guarded her wisdom well and told you what you would know. She prophesied the future, but there is another prophesy running alongside the one she spoke of, and only one will be to your liking. Ponder that, My Lord, through the ages of your imprisonment."

"What other prophecy do you speak of?"

She said no more, but turned and walked from him.

He shouted again, his voice booming, "What other prophecy!"

But though they were close together many times in the years to come, as she directed the building of his barrow and the labyrinth that led to it, she never spoke another word to Lorcan Labraid. Her victory over him was almost complete, though she still had one last act to perform.

And thereafter, she knew that Labraid's ultimate fate lay not in her hands, but in those of the one who was yet to come.

19

They walked through the entrance hall unchallenged, the old house feeling almost as empty as the new one, perhaps more so with its absence of spirits. And in his thoughts, Will echoed Harriet's wish, that Henry had also walked after death, or that he might have left word of his discoveries behind him.

They made their way to the chapel, but as they opened the door on to the dark interior, it was Eloise who said, "We should go and look for Sophie. She's almost on her own this weekend and she'll be wondering where we are." She saw Will's reluctance. "You don't trust her. Of course you don't – she's appeared on the radar out of nowhere, and the shapeshifter doesn't like her."

Will shook his head, wondering if Eloise was expressing her own doubts as much as guessing at his.

"It's not that I don't trust her. I will admit, the shapeshifter's dislike of her is confusing, but I've hypnotised her twice now and seen nothing to suggest she wishes me ill."

"Then what is it?"

"I wish I could say, but I don't know."

"So let's go and get her. She'll either be in the Heston common room or in her own room." As they started walking, Eloise said idly, "Of course, it's possible she's been put here to harm you, but doesn't know it. Actually, the same could be said of me."

"I don't follow," said Will.

"Think about it. Wyndham is old, right? We know he's a couple of hundred years old, and unlike you, he hasn't spent half of that time hibernating . . ."

"He would have had to sleep though."

"Quite true, but he also doesn't have the restrictions on his movements that you do. He can travel, make friends, study, learn, in ways that have been closed to you. So if he knew that you'd one day re-emerge, and if he knew that one day you'd have to come to Marland, he could have been influencing people from birth, hypnotising them, maybe even hypnotising their parents, creating a kind of army of sleeper agents. And the real beauty is, they might not even know themselves that that's what they are. Like I said, for all I know, I could be one of them. I could be thinking I'm part of your destiny, and actually I'm part of Wyndham's plan to destroy you."

"He hasn't demonstrated a high opinion of you the two times we've spoken."

"An act. He doesn't want to give me away."

"And you were unfriendly to me when I first met you. If I hadn't rescued you from that gang, you might never have befriended me."

"A gang which included Marcus, who subsequently came here as Wyndham's spy. I mean, how did Wyndham even know about Marcus?" She stopped, suddenly enthused by what had seemed like idle speculation a few moments before. "Will, think of all the things that have fallen into place, think of Jex and me and the pendant, and the gang with Marcus in it and now Sophie. God, even Harriet is a ghost who was first raised in our presence by Wyndham. So many coincidences – don't you think it suggests a guiding hand, someone who might have orchestrated it all?"

Will nodded his agreement, but said, "He is certainly powerful, and his involvement is probably more subtle and more complex than we realise, but if he was the puppet-master you portray, would he not have found it easier to destroy me than he actually has?" She made to reply, but he continued, "And there is another explanation for what appears coincidental – destiny. If anything, destiny might have run more smoothly, and created greater coincidences still, had it not been for Wyndham's attempts to interfere with it."

"Yes, I suppose that's true."

"And think back on the way he acted with Elfleda and with Edgar – I don't think he ever fully understood them. But you're right, it's quite possible that he's had an influence on people, including Sophie, who are quite unaware of that influence."

"What about me?"

"No, you are true. I know it, and so does Wyndham."

She smiled and they started on their way along the corridor again, when Eloise said, "Can I ask you something, about Sophie? Not that it matters or anything."

Will looked at her and knew what the question was, one spurred by their brief, sad conversation with Rachel.

"No, she doesn't carry the line." For all her claims that it didn't matter, Eloise looked relieved. Will said, "It's not something I can explain fully. In the past of course I just thought my instincts discounted some people and selected others, usually based on health and youth alone. Even now, I'm only just beginning to recognise the differences in scents." He laughed.

Eloise said, "What's funny?"

"Only that I've lived for nearly eight centuries knowing almost nothing, and have now learned it all in a few months, when . . ."

"When nothing. We have no idea what will happen tomorrow."

He looked at her and nodded, conceding that at least.

When they reached the Heston House common room, Eloise looked in first, then opened the door more widely once she realised no one else was in there. Sophie was reading what looked to be a substantial letter, but she looked up now and smiled warmly.

"Hello! I've been looking for you."

"We had to go into the city," said Eloise. "Is anyone else still in the school?"

Sophie said, "Just us. James and Lottie Smith were meant to be staying, but left at the last minute. Miss Lawrence and Miss Bettencourt are here, but otherwise it's just you and me." She looked at Will, her eyes more piercing in some way as she said, "And you of course."

"Except I'm not really here."

"Which brings me to this," said Sophie, brandishing the letter. Will and Eloise crossed the room and sat down opposite her. "I've had a letter about you, from someone called Phillip Wyndham, but how on earth does he or anyone else know that I've met you? It's all terribly strange, don't you think?"

Eloise threw a glance at Will, as if to suggest this latest development supported her theory. "What does it say?"

"*Dear Miss Hamilton, you do not know me, but I write in your best interests. I am aware that you will have made some new friends recently, one of whom will call himself Will or William, the other being a fellow pupil at the school. I have no doubt that they have charmed you and that you are eager to help them in their endeavours, but before you proceed further, I would like to provide you with some background information on one of them in particular.*" Sophie leafed through the three sheets of paper, saying, "Then he basically goes on to tell me that you're a vampire, that you're eight hundred years old, and that if you're not stopped or killed in the next few days . . . let me get this right." She studied the final sheet, looking for the exact words. "That's it . . . *evil will triumph and the world as we know it will cease to exist.*"

Will wondered what Wyndham was up to. The letter seemed rather desperate. Edgar had assured Will that Wyndham would be weakened if they burned his house, but to this extent? Could he really be reduced to sending letters to sully Will's reputation?

Of course, the implication was that Will would be damaged without Sophie's support, but this could be a bluff, a double or even triple bluff. Perhaps it served no other purpose than to lull Will into a false sense of security by feigning desperation.

Sophie looked up, smiling, and when neither of them responded, she turned to Eloise and said, "Did you know about this?"

"Yes. Yes, I did."

Sophie laughed. "OK, firstly, why do I believe it? I mean, seriously, vampires, and evil, and . . . But there's the thing, because I do believe it, I know it's true. So secondly, why am I not completely freaked out by it? You're a vampire. Why am I not freaked . . . actually, why am I not freaked out by any of what's happened?"

"I hypnotised you."

She stared at Will for a moment, then shook her head.

"Only to lessen the shock of what you've experienced, and the effect will wear off little by little." At least, he thought it would.

Sophie looked at Eloise, who shrugged nonchalantly, as if to suggest this was quite normal.

"Well, I don't remember you hypnotising me. But I suppose that's the point, isn't it?"

"I think so." Will pointed at the letter. "Does the name Phillip Wyndham mean anything to you?"

"No. I thought it rang a bell when I first saw it, but I can't think where from." She turned to Eloise and said, "Oh, cook left sandwiches and cakes in the dining room for us. They'll do the same tomorrow, a hot lunch and then sandwiches later."

"Thanks," said Eloise, bemused.

Will said, "You should eat, both of you."

"I've already had mine," said Sophie. "Don't worry,

I've left you loads. I don't suppose you eat food, Will?"

"No, I don't."

"So . . ."

Before she could ask the next question Eloise stood up and said, "Sophie, I think I will have something to eat now. Come with me and I'll fill you in on Will and everything else." Eloise looked fleetingly at Will who nodded his approval.

Sophie said, "Good. Coming, Will?"

"No, I'll meet you in the chapel."

Will waited for them to leave, then took a look round the room, imagining how it was for them, their home from home, the place where they belonged. He walked to the broken window and pushed it open, looking out on to the park which was now empty, though he knew they were out there, all those creatures that waited to do his bidding.

He closed the window again and strolled along towards the chapel. Before he'd reached the doors, he heard voices nearby and took a detour. Two female teachers were in one of the offices near the headmaster's. Presumably Miss Lawrence and Miss Bettencourt, Will recognised the voice of one as the young teacher he'd occasionally seen talking on her phone outside in the evenings.

He heard the other one say, "He never struck me as

the suicidal type. Mind you, have to admit I never really liked him very much. And I know you shouldn't speak ill of the dead."

"I didn't teach him," said the younger teacher.

"Not a difficult boy, just full of himself. Still, I guess he might have grown out of it."

Will retreated and made his way into the chapel. It was so still in there that it was hard to believe a battle of any description lay ahead. There was no doubting it though, and the only way it might be prevented was if he found the gate before tomorrow night.

With that in mind, he made his way to the small door opposite the vestry and put his hand over the lock, feeling the mechanism slowly yielding. It clicked open, but at the same time the chapel door opened and closed and Sophie stepped inside on her own.

She couldn't see at first, as bright as it appeared in Will's eyes, but she walked forward confidently anyway and then caught sight of him and smiled.

"Eloise said she had something to do, but I'm glad we've got a chance to talk privately. She told me everything by the way, or a quick version anyway." She became distracted by the realisation of where he was standing, and said, "Oh, so you do think my little storeroom is the place?"

Will was struggling to keep up, as if she was speaking

in another language, but latched on to the final comment and said, "I think it the most likely, though I can find no sign of the secret passage I'm looking for."

Sophie was standing right in front of him now and smiled as she said, "I did wonder at the way you speak. And for the record, I know you're in love with Eloise and that's great, but I think there's something terribly attractive about . . . you know."

He didn't, and wasn't sure that he wanted to find out more, so he smiled in acknowledgement and said, "Was that what you wanted to discuss in private?"

"No, of course not, and I'm not saying it's . . . No, it's about the letter this guy sent me, and about you. 'You need the boy, the boy needs you.' Ring any bells?"

Her eyes were dazzlingly intense and there was something driven in them now, as if the letter from Wyndham had achieved the very opposite of what the sorcerer had hoped for. And again, Will had to admit to himself, he had little idea of Wyndham's real intentions in sending that letter.

Even before he replied, he knew she would not be easily dissuaded, but still he said, "Yes, you told me a clairvoyant had spoken those words to you, but even if we are to believe the outpourings of clairvoyants, and you yourself described it as meaningless, what reason do we have to believe . . ."

"Because I know. I knew the moment I met you there was something and that letter just confirmed it. I'm not a girl with a crush, Will, I have no desire to replace Eloise, and she's very sweet. But I know I have a role to play in this, whatever this is, and that role is at your side."

"Then you know more than me, for I do not know what even my own role is."

Sophie smiled, full of strength and confidence, and for the first time he could picture her easily as a queen, but also for the first time he could imagine how driven that queen would be, how intent on destroying everything that didn't yield to her dominion. Was that why the shapeshifter disliked her? Was her potential disturbing even to the denizens of the underworld?

"I don't want you to worry about this, Will. There's going to be a battle, and I'm not at all afraid. You'll see."

The chapel door opened and Eloise stepped inside. Sophie didn't turn, and wouldn't have been able to see her if she had, but she seemed to know instinctively that it was Eloise and she looked up at Will and put her finger to her lips. As she lowered it again, there was that smile. There had been such a subtle yet terrible transformation in this girl that Will would have believed it an act had he not seen a premonition of it, a premonition which he had himself induced.

20

Eloise was carrying something cumbersome and Will went to her. He expected Sophie to follow, but he heard her push open the storeroom door behind him and then felt his eyes smart as she turned on the light in there.

Eloise said, "It's from the Great Hall, our dining room. I hope I've selected the best one – there were a few to choose from. And then I nearly ran into Miss Bettencourt on the way out. Not sure how I would have explained that."

She removed the cloth that covered it and with an effort held up what she was carrying – armour that glinted in the moonlight coming through the windows. Will took it off her and smiled as he looked at it. It was a breastplate and backplate linked together.

"It's called a cuirass."

"Did you have these in your childhood?"

He shook his head, smiling, and said, "And I think I predate this one in particular by about four hundred years."

"The thing is, if we don't make it through the gateway and there is a battle, Wyndham will target your heart – he's bound to – so I thought you could wear this under your coat. There's another one that would protect your neck too, but I couldn't get to it, and I'm not sure how comfortable it would've been."

"Thank you, but won't this be missed?"

"On Monday probably, but we'll put it back before that if all goes well. And . . ." She hesitated. "You know, the school isn't completely empty. There are still two teachers here. I'm just wondering – it doesn't matter what form it takes, a battle is quite a big thing, isn't it, not something that can happen without people noticing?"

"You're quite right. I suspect a misplaced piece of armour is of little consequence. I'll put it in the crypt for now." He started to turn, but stopped short and spoke more quietly as he said, "Have you noticed a change in Sophie, perhaps since she received that letter?"

"I didn't know her that well to begin with. Yes, her behaviour's a little bit off in some way, but I guessed that's because you've hypnotised her. And if that's what it does to people, I kind of feel sorry for all those taxi drivers." Will laughed and Eloise laughed a little too as she said, "All I'll say is, when I was giving her a potted history of you and our whole . . . thing, she looked . . .

She looked like she was getting fired up, you know, with adrenaline or whatever."

"I thought the same," said Will, but left it at that. "I'll put this in the crypt. Sophie's in the storeroom."

He walked down to the crypt, but thought better of leaving the armour in the open, even there, even with the school empty, and walked on to the ossuary. He placed it on the floor, but as he did so noticed that his familiar skull had turned fractionally again, looking off to one side rather than towards the door.

He straightened it, but at the same time he looked up at the ceiling and listened, to the gentle vibration of Sophie and Eloise talking quietly to each other. He wondered how close the ossuary was to the storeroom, and wondered in turn if this skull was moving because of something they were doing in the room above. Not that he was certain how that would help in the search now. All in all, there were hundreds of skeletons here, piled up tightly in patterns of different bones – skulls here, femurs there, vertebrae here, ribs there.

And though his familiar skull was loose in its place, most of the others would not be. So even in the unlikely event that the bare walls of the ossuary might reveal something about the gateway, removing the bones would be a week's work, a week he did not have.

No, he had one chance only and that was to invest

his time in the storeroom. If there was no door hidden behind those wooden panels, if it was not the location of the second gateway, then the battle would not be avoided.

He left and joined the other two, and as he approached the storeroom, he heard Eloise saying, "Not when he hibernates, but he has these sort of waking dreams."

Will smiled, finding it odd to hear Eloise talking about him to someone else. Less odd was Sophie's natural curiosity, but Will's smile fell away when he thought of what underpinned that curiosity, her conviction that she had a vital part to play in his story. Though she had not voiced it, she was vying to be the one chosen, to be queen of a kingdom over which he didn't want to reign.

Sophie replied to Eloise, saying, "And what does he dream about, as if I can't guess?"

It was Eloise who sounded effortlessly regal now as she said, "Do you really think you or I could second-guess the thoughts of someone who's lived for over seven hundred and fifty years?"

"I see what you mean," said Sophie, chastened. "I keep forgetting."

Will pushed the door open and found them on opposite walls, idly exploring the panels, looking for hidden catches that he already knew they wouldn't find.

183

They both turned to look at him, but he had a sudden realisation of what he needed to do.

"I'll be back in a moment."

He went back to the crypt and took one of the swords, though not the one he'd felt so confident using for combat – he didn't want to use that weapon for what he had in mind now. Nor did he want to use the knife he carried in his pocket, the blade of which he considered too terrible and too sacred to be used for anything else.

When he got back to them, he closed the door and looked around the room. It was as Eloise had said: when set against a possible battle, missing armour and minor damage counted for little. But the realisation had come when he'd seen them searching for a secret way to get beyond those panels, when there was a much simpler method.

Eloise said, "What are you doing, Will?"

"Finding out what Henry wanted to hide behind this wood panelling."

He chose the wall behind the altar first, reckoning on it being a likely spot for a passage descending beneath the chapel. He placed the sword tip in the corner of one of the panel squares and slowly drove it in, the wood splintering around the force of the blade.

He stopped as soon as the sword was through the wood and into the cavity beyond, then slowly pulled it along the side of the square, splinters of wood flying off under the pressure of the metal cutting edge. He wondered at one point if the blade itself might snap, but these four swords seemed to have been forged in the same foundry as Will and his kind – they didn't break easily.

Once he'd reached the next corner, he pushed the blade in again and worked up the side of the square. He was conscious of Eloise and Sophie watching him the whole time. Eloise had a look of concern about her, as if fearing the consequences of this much damage and the attention it would bring. Sophie looked on with barely concealed excitement – if she'd had a sword in her hand, he had no doubt she'd have joined in.

Will reached the end of the final side and the square panel creaked and yielded to gravity, dropping out on to the floor with a dull clatter. Will looked at the exposed wall beyond. Eloise stepped closer too. But it was Sophie who spoke as she peered into the cavity.

"Oh my God, that's amazing! Why on earth was it covered up?"

Again her tone was all excitement, the thrill of someone seeing something she'd never encountered before. Will and Eloise stood by with the measured response of people all too familiar with the paintings and the runic writing that filled the section of wall he'd exposed, and who looked at it with mixed feelings.

Will said, "Well at least it seems we're looking in the right place."

Eloise nodded but looked a little confused as she said, "You think this was part of a building that was here before the house? Or maybe Henry had a copy made."

"I think it more likely that this has been transplanted. Perhaps it was unearthed as the foundations were laid for this house, or perhaps these walls had once been hidden within the monastery itself."

The latter thought, together with the memory of his family's close ties with Marland Abbey long before this house had existed, was both intriguing and disturbing to Will. He imagined his father being taken in secret to view these paintings, just as he might have been taken to see the labyrinth.

The troubling question was whether Will's father had known about his son's part in all this, and if so, in how much detail. Had he known that Will's mother would be killed? Had he known that Will himself would be attacked on the night the witches burned? In his heart, he hoped it was not so, but almost dared not think about it, and felt guilty for tarnishing the memory of a man he had never thought ill of before.

Sophie looked taken aback and said, "Why aren't you two as excited by this as I am?" The understanding hit her even before she'd finished asking the question, and instantly she pointed and said, "You've seen something like this before!"

Eloise said, "There's a labyrinth beneath the old abbey, or there was – most of it's been destroyed now – and the walls are covered with paintings like this."

"When you say destroyed . . ."

"Wyndham destroyed it," said Will, backing up Eloise's small lie. "It contained a gateway that was meant for me, which is why he destroyed it. What we're searching for here is the second gateway."

Sophie smiled, her eyes full of passion as she said, "Where does it lead to?"

"We don't know, we only have ideas, but we have too little time to go into it now."

Undeterred, Sophie said, "The underworld – you're looking for the gate into the underworld." She pressed her head sideways into the cavity and said, "You need to cut away more of these panels."

Will glanced at Eloise, who looked full of misgivings, and as Sophie stepped away again, he cut sideways from the top of the square, driving the sword through the panels and the thicker supports. He forced another cut from the bottom corner of the existing hole and then pulled the damaged section, peeling it away until it cracked and splintered and broke free.

There was a substantial section exposed now, but one large picture in particular was visible, right in the centre of the wall. It was a desolate scene of devastation. There were no creatures here, only ruins and flames, and sitting imperious in the middle of it all, a king and queen on two thrones.

The features were simply rendered, but there was no doubting the king was a likeness of Will, no less so than the one he'd seen in the labyrinth. Beyond being fair, the identity of the queen might have been more open to interpretation, but all three of them stared in silence, not needing to voice the fact of which they were all certain, that it represented Sophie.

21

"I knew it. I don't know how, but seriously, I just knew." Sophie was talking to them, but she couldn't take her eyes off the image in front of her.

Will looked at Eloise – it was as if, in removing the panelling, Will had destroyed everything she'd come to believe in. He shook his head, trying to assure her that he didn't accept this, that he wouldn't. All she could do was offer a weak smile in response.

Will was about to suggest that the other walls might yield more, even as he held out no hope of finding paintings that would reassure Eloise. She'd firmly believed from the outset that he had goodness within him and that he could make this end well. He saw little chance of such a view being portrayed here.

So it was with some relief that he heard the chapel door opening and a voice call out, "Hello?"

It was the young teacher, and he guessed that he'd created more disturbance with the cutting and breaking of the panelled wall than he'd thought.

Quietly he said, "Someone's heard the noise, one of your teachers. I'll have to turn the light out – stay quiet."

Before they could respond he moved to the door, switched off the light, then put his hand over the lock and worked the mechanism closed. He stood then, listening, to the uneven breathing of the two girls in the room, to the barely audible steps in the chapel.

The teacher had sounded nervous, even afraid, and he was surprised at first that she continued to advance, but then the explanation came as the other teacher's voice was heard, saying, "It's probably nothing, Lucy – you know how the place creaks and groans when it's empty."

"You're probably right," said the younger one, her voice much closer, suggesting her colleague had stayed by the door. "I'll check the vestry though. Anyone could stroll in here with the place like this."

"So do you really think it wise to disturb them?"

"Oh, Miriam!" Will could hear her now on the other side of the door. The vestry door opened, a light was turned on, showing under the storeroom door. The movement was reversed and then a second later she tried the storeroom door. Her voice was shockingly close as she said, "No one here, so I think we can sleep safe in our beds. Unless of course . . . should I check the crypt?"

"Oh, please don't . . ." The younger teacher laughed and was already walking back to her colleague. But then the older teacher said, "As a matter of fact, I think we should check on our girls."

"Do you think we ought?"

No more was said and the chapel door closed. Will turned the light on, screwing his eyes shut as he put on his dark glasses. They were both looking at him, still projecting opposing sentiments.

Will didn't think they'd heard the final exchange and said, "I think you should go. Your teachers are going to check on you now."

Eloise nodded, looking as relieved as Will felt, that they wouldn't have to explore these walls any further together.

Sophie was searching for some reason to stay, but in the end could only muster, "But we haven't finished."

"I can work through the night, more quietly. We can scarcely afford to arouse the suspicions of your teachers now, so do not return until tomorrow after lunch, and be much in evidence during the morning."

Eloise said, "Will's right. Come on, we should go." She glanced once more at the picture on the wall and tried a good-humoured shrug, but he could tell that it had wounded her, and though it had nothing to do with him, he couldn't help but feel responsible for that hurt.

"I won't be able to sleep," said Sophie. "But I suppose you're right."

She looked at Will, an expression that was determined to be intimate, as if they both knew that they had things to discuss without Eloise there. Will walked them through the chapel and after bidding them goodnight, he locked the main door behind them. If he'd believed Eloise might visit him later he would have taken the risk and left it open, but he did not want to see Sophie again tonight.

Once back in the storeroom, he worked methodically from the section he'd already uncovered, cutting the panels away slowly and stacking them until he'd reached the corner. The whole of the wall backing on to the altar was exposed now, with the royal portrait of desolation as the centrepiece.

He started on the wall at the end of the room and was aware of his own reluctance as he reached the middle section and found the beginnings of a large central picture. It was almost a relief when he finally revealed it, a copy of the picture he'd seen in the circular chamber of the labyrinth, of Will sitting alone on a throne, atop a hill of mutilated bodies.

He cut the panelling from the rest of the wall before returning to it. And this time he saw something he hadn't noticed before, and wondered if he had missed the same detail on the picture in the labyrinth. On either side of his head, the throne had two letters carved into it, W and E. The hope it caused to spring up in him was short-lived because she was quite clearly not there with him, and because he would not wish Eloise to be part of such a picture anyway.

He'd been working for several hours now and was surprised that he hadn't heard the chapel door being tried. Perhaps the teachers were already asleep up on the top floor, but he thought it unlikely that Sophie or Eloise were resting easily, the one full of nervous excitement, the other of dread.

He started on the third wall, slowly working from the back corner towards the front of the room. He'd developed a system by now, for cutting away the panels, easing them free, piling them on the floor, and he moved quickly along to the middle of the wall, to the point facing the depiction of Will and Sophie.

He'd only revealed a part of it when he realised it was of Eloise and he pressed onwards, determined to find a mirror of the scene opposite. His eagerness fell away though, as more of the picture became visible, and once it was all in view, he took a step back and stared at it with a heaviness inside him.

It was Eloise, but standing alone, a sword held upright in one hand, a skull in the other. As simply as it was painted, her expression was clear, one of grim determination. Eloise as death, an image he still couldn't reconcile in his mind with the Eloise he knew.

Reluctantly, for want of knowing what else to do, Will continued to remove the panels, and only then, near the end of that side of the room, did he find a hint of what he'd been looking for. The panelling had something else built into it, a system of bolts locking it into the floor and ceiling, but not in any way he could fully understand as he took it apart.

He'd felt no mechanism there when he'd searched, and yet he could see clearly now that the wall had contained a door, seamlessly hidden. More troubling still, the painted wall beyond showed no sign of a door either.

He ran his hands along the paint-covered surface, unable to sense any mechanism within it, unable to find even the suggestion of an opening. He tapped on the stones, but they sounded solid, too solid for him to break through even if there was a door there.

He stood with his hands resting on the wall, and he cursed Henry, his brother's clever descendant, who'd deciphered so much of this mystery only to wrap it in riddles of his own design. He cursed Wyndham who'd thrown obstacles in his path at every opportunity, to the extent that a battle of any description was more preferable now than the frustration Will had become used to.

Most of all he cursed himself and he cursed his distant ancestor, Lorcan Labraid, who presumably was still somewhere to be found beyond this hidden gateway. He cursed him because there were three pictures on the walls around Will, pictures that he imagined were meant to depict his possible futures, none of which he wanted.

Would it not be better, for him and his family and the honour and esteem that had once been associated with their name, that he die on the battlefield? Even if it was seven centuries too late, even if it was a battlefield of Wyndham's creation, surely that had to be better than the dark future laid out before him on these walls?

He left the room, but before he closed the door, he pulled the light switch from the wall, tearing the cable which sparked and died. Then he locked the door, determined that neither Sophie nor Eloise would see this room again, or at least not until they'd discovered the secret of how to pass through it.

He walked out through the chapel, opening the door and moving on through the school. It was four in the morning, much later than he'd realised. They would be asleep now, even Sophie, but it was odd walking through the school which usually contained so much life, but which now had only four beating hearts within it.

When he reached her door, he could hear Eloise

moaning quietly in her sleep, muttering broken words. So the dreams had still not ceased, or they had returned. He eased the door open and stepped inside, and felt himself immediately calmed by her presence, by her scent, by the very humanity of her. He put the scarf over the lamp, as she always did for him, then turned it on. And when he looked at her, she was calm and her eyes were open.

"I'm sorry to disturb you."

As if accepting now that he was really there, she rubbed her eyes and sat up in the bed. "I'm not. Sit down." She patted the bed and Will sat on it facing her, and took her hand in his. Her skin was hot to the touch. Her face darkened a little as she remembered the previous evening and said, "Did you find anything else, on the walls?"

"More pictures, another that could be me, one that could be you, all as nonsensical as the first."

"That was definitely Sophie. There was something about that picture that was just her. As your queen."

Will squeezed her hand. "It could just as easily be a warning as a premonition, warning me that nothing will come of my association with Sophie."

Eloise smiled, seeing through his diplomacy, and said, "What about the picture of me, what did that show?"

"You were alone, just as I was on the neighbouring wall."

"Oh." She looked confused, trying to extract a meaning from that.

"Eloise, it means nothing. Do the murals and carvings in cathedrals depict God as he is, angels, saints, heaven and hell? No, they depict what the men of that time imagined. And the paintings we saw tonight and in the labyrinth, they were not the work of some divine or even demonic hand, but of men trying to explain mysteries only partly understood."

"Nice try." She smiled. "But I'll accept you're right in one respect. If those paintings don't depict anything good then they're meaningless because you're good, and even now, even after . . ." She stumbled, he suspected over the thought of Sophie's emergence as a rival who would grow in strength. "I still believe this can end well, that it must."

He nodded. "What if I had not set across the park to check the new house? What if I hadn't met her? For seven centuries there were no coincidences, but now . . . it's like a watch mechanism, as if the cog with my life on it has slipped into place, interlocking with all the others."

"But that's how we met, remember?"

"True, and no matter what ancient peoples painted on their walls, I know my own heart. I wish I could be as confident that this will end well, but it will end with us together." He held up the pendant hanging from his neck. "I am the West, you are the East, I am the Moon and you are the Sun. You have no rival."

Eloise smiled. "Coming from any other boy that would sound really cheesy. But thank you." She brushed his cheek, then lay down again. "Would you stay for a while?"

Will knew what she meant, to watch over her while she slept, as he had done those weeks beneath the cathedral. He turned off the lamp and sat back on the edge of the bed and stroked her hair until he sensed that she had fallen asleep.

Still he didn't move, and only stirred when he sensed the paling of the darkness beyond the curtains. Even then he left reluctantly. He stood at the door, looking at Eloise sleeping there, forever unattainable. And when he finally turned away, he caught a glimpse of himself in the mirror and felt a seething contempt for the person he saw looking back.

22

Will stayed in the crypt through the rest of the night and the morning. He worked on the armour, moulding and shaping it until it felt comfortable when he wore it beneath his coat. Then he put it back in the ossuary with the swords and sat outside reading over Harriet's journals once more.

Eloise and Sophie kept their word and did not come to see him before lunch. But he expected them to appear immediately afterwards and was surprised when they didn't. The afternoon was pressing on when he finally heard the chapel door opening.

He stood, slipping the journals into his pockets, and edged back towards the ossuary door, but stopped as he heard Sophie say in a whisper, "He might be in the storeroom."

Eloise didn't respond, but a moment later their footsteps sounded as they descended to the crypt. Will walked out to meet them and made a point of embracing Eloise while saying casually over her shoulder, "Hello, Sophie."

"Hello." To her credit, she didn't appear snubbed and, if anything, seemed more curious about the dynamics of his relationship with Eloise.

As Eloise stepped back again, she said, "Sorry we're late, Lawrence and Bettencourt were all over us."

"Unbelievable," said Sophie. "Bettencourt even asked if we wanted to go for a walk with them, as it's such a beautiful day."

"Is it very beautiful?" asked Will? Sophie looked concerned, as if worried she'd been insensitive. Eloise simply nodded. "Then the full moon will be all the brighter tonight."

"We still have time," said Eloise.

Latching on to that, Sophie was enthusiastic as she said, "Yes, do tell, what did you find on the other walls?"

"Paintings, but nothing of . . ."

"Can we see?"

Will laughed away the interruption and glanced towards the crypt steps, saying, "It's possible that with some difficulty I could move through the chapel, but even if I endured the discomfort involved, the electric lights in the storeroom are no longer working. And there is nothing worthwhile to see, nothing that you haven't seen already."

Sophie seemed to read something into his final comment, perhaps assuming that he was attaching particular significance to the picture of them together. He didn't bother to correct her because it was the least of their concerns.

"I found a sort of door in the wooden panelling as I took it apart, with a mechanism like none I've ever seen, but the wall beyond it was a smooth surface, with no opening at all that was visible."

"Do you think it could still be the gateway? After all, the one in the labyrinth didn't have an actual opening – it was just a plain floor."

Will thought back to the ghost of his mother, descending into the floor of that round chamber as if down a spiralling stone staircase. Eloise could well be right, but of course, that only raised another issue – they had also never learned how to open that gateway, let alone this one.

Will looked at the ceiling and said, "So many coincidences and so few of any use."

Sophie looked confused, but Eloise laughed, understanding his frustration immediately. But it was Sophie who said, "You need Dr Higson, don't you, to tell you how this gateway is opened?"

"We think we need him. We're making an assumption that he would have been with Wyndham."

"Well, there you are. I heard Bettencourt saying they're expecting him back any moment. So that gives you a couple of hours before it gets dark. I have to admit, I kind of like the idea of a battle, but surely an hour or so should be enough to get the information out of him, get the gate opened and . . . do whatever it is you have to do."

Eloise said, "You forget, until it gets dark, Will can't exactly go and knock on Higson's door."

"So I'll lure him down here."

Will was impressed by her confidence, by the way no problem appeared insurmountable to her.

"Wyndham knows who you are," said Will.

"Apparently so, but that doesn't mean he's told the head. Higson's been off visiting Alex's family. And you know what, if he does know about me and doesn't take the bait, what of it? We'll lose a couple of hours at most because as soon as it gets dark, you can go and find him anyway. But isn't it worth the risk?"

"Yes, you're right," said Will.

Eloise said, "It's a slim chance, but if it does work it'll give us some breathing space."

"Good, so we just wait for him to get back." Then, no doubt thinking of where Higson was returning from, Sophie said, "Poor Alex. You have to wonder why he did it, don't you? What on earth could have been going through his mind?"

Will and Eloise looked at each other with horror, as

Will realised this had not been part of Eloise's account to Sophie, and that she hadn't jumped to the most natural conclusion given what else she'd learned.

After what felt like a dizzying pause, Will said, "So, what did you do to occupy yourselves through this morning?"

Sophie raised her eyebrows. "You wouldn't *believe* how tortuous it was." Eloise joined in, the two of them taking it in turns, sometimes talking over each other, to explain the drudgeries of a single morning spent in the company of two teachers.

It was Eloise talking when Will heard a car approach and stop somewhere behind the school.

He put his hand up. "A car just arrived."

Sophie said, "I'll go and see if it's him. Get ready though – I'll get him to the top of the crypt steps, but you might have to pounce from there."

Will laughed. "I'll be ready."

With that, Sophie made a swift departure and the two of them stood, facing each other in silent anticipation.

It was a few minutes before Eloise said, "Do you think you should get a sword?"

"Not for Higson." Will looked at the crypt steps, the light filtering down from the chapel above. "She'll have to get him to the top of the steps – do you think she could persuade him?"

Eloise gave a wry smile. "Like I said, I didn't really know her before, but one thing I did know, she was always that kind of girl, you know – confident, got whatever she wanted."

She'd sounded expansive, but came to a sudden stop, as if only now appreciating how those same qualities might play out in the near future.

Will put his hand on Eloise's shoulder and said, "You have no rival." She laughed, and then Will was surprised to hear two voices approaching the chapel.

The first was Higson, saying, "Can't it wait, Sophie? I've just had the most horrendous journey."

Then Sophie, chatty, insistent, innocuous, saying, "Poor you, I can only imagine how awful it must have been. Were they terribly shaken? Of course they were, what a stupid thing to say. I can't stop thinking of poor Alex. But actually, yes, I think this probably is important. I definitely heard water dripping. No, not dripping, like a constant trickle."

The chapel door opened. Eloise held her breath. Will moved and stood just around the corner from the bottom of the steps. He glanced up – the light would be uncomfortable, possibly even cause a little blistering, but it would be worth the pain if it meant snaring Higson.

"What were you doing in the chapel anyway?"

Sophie sounded appropriately subdued, even

embarrassed, as she said, "Praying. We were good friends."

It was a great act, distracting Higson from the truth of an impending ambush enough that he kept walking as he said, "Of course, sorry, I didn't mean to suggest . . ." Then he stopped. "So, where did you hear this leak?"

"If you stand over here," said Sophie, appearing now at the top of the steps. "I don't think it's coming from down in the crypt. I think it's coming from that wall there."

Will peered round and saw her pointing at the wall above the crypt steps. He moved back again as Higson's footsteps approached.

There was a moment of silence and then Higson said, "I don't hear anything, Sophie."

"You need to move closer. I can hear it quite clearly from here."

"But I'm only . . ." He stopped, a pause loaded with calculation and understanding. The tone of his voice had changed completely when he said, "Oh, Sophie, not you too!"

"Dr Higson, wait . . ."

Will sprang up and ventured part of the way up the steps. Sophie had grabbed hold of Higson, but the headmaster immediately flung her away, and ran back along the aisle. He'd been too far away to begin with and ran too quickly for Will to have even a hope of catching him. The chapel door slammed open as Higson careered through it.

Sophie recovered herself quickly and said, "I'll see where he goes."

"Be careful!"

She was already running towards the chapel door and was through it and gone. Will stepped back into the shade, frustrated now, even though he'd held out little hope, because Sophie had so very nearly made a success of it. He looked at Eloise and said, "She was so close to snaring him."

"I heard. She's quite remarkable, isn't she?"

"If only he knew that I have no desire to kill him."

"Yeah, probably a bit late for that. And for all we know, he fears Wyndham more than he fears you."

"For all we know, he's right to do so."

He heard Sophie's footsteps hurrying back, the chapel door opening. She walked quickly up the aisle, stopping only to pick something up, keys which she held up as she reached the bottom of the steps.

"I wondered why he didn't just get in his car – he must have dropped them as he was breaking free from me."

"Where did he go?"

"He went running across the park, off towards the

new house. Why do you think he went there?"

"Panic," said Will, and thought back to his first meeting with Sophie. "If he stays at the house till after dark, we might still have a chance. If he calls for a taxi from there, then there's little hope."

Sophie said, "Maybe we could go after him, Eloise and me. We could . . ."

"Absolutely not," said Will. "You know him as your headmaster, but you know nothing else about him, nor the things of which he might be capable."

Eloise said, "We just have to wait."

"Yes, but it would be useful between now and nightfall if you go back above and keep watch, make certain he doesn't return. If he doesn't, then I will go to the new house as soon as it's safe for me to do so."

"We could take it in turns to watch," said Sophie. Her implication was clear, that the other could keep Will company.

He smiled, but was firm as he said, "Better that you keep each other company. I have things I must do. Alone."

It was settled and they left shortly afterwards. In truth, Will had nothing to do, but after so detesting his solitude for so long, he wanted to be alone for a little while, to take stock, to prepare himself.

Although he'd wanted to sound purposeful and

optimistic for their benefit, he saw little chance now of accessing the gateway before Wyndham commenced battle. With that in mind, he retrieved his armour and sword from the ossuary. He put on the armour and checked once more that it didn't hinder his movement with the weapon. Not that he knew if armour and a sword would be of any use in the battle to come. The only thing Will knew for certain was Wyndham's determination that the battle would end with Will destroyed or disabled.

He stood then, near the bottom of the crypt steps, staring up at the weakening light coming through the stained-glass windows. And he felt it as a physical sensation, a beautiful coolness seeping into his skin, when the sun finally slipped below the horizon.

Almost instantly he heard footsteps and the chapel door open, and Eloise's voice. "Will?"

He leapt up the steps and said, "Is he there?"

"No, but the sun's set and the moon's low in the sky. If we're going to get to the new house before . . . well, before whatever, we need to go."

"I'll fetch my sword."

"Oh, Sophie said could you bring one for her too."

Will nodded, but thought of Marcus, who'd wielded a sword so expertly, so bravely, and yet it had not been enough to save him. Would he be consigning Sophie to the same fate if he allowed her to fight? Perhaps not, and he wished he had more time to contemplate why the thought of arming her filled him with such unease. But ironically, the one thing he did not have was more time.

23

Will ran the few steps to the ossuary, opened the bundle of swords and, as the three that remained were of a similar size and weight, chose the first that came to hand. He turned to leave then, but laughed a little to himself as he saw that his familiar skull had moved once again.

He stopped, though he knew Eloise was waiting for him, and straightened it. But as he did so, one of the bones across the room moved and another fell on to the floor. Will walked over and looked at the spot from which the bone had fallen. The others appeared and felt tightly packed, but even as he looked, another bone was dislodged somewhere behind him and fell to the floor.

Will crouched down and felt the floor, trying to sense if there was any movement in the stones, any vibration that might be causing this. There wasn't and he stared at the walls of deconstructed skeletons and felt chilled in some way.

Another movement in the wall behind him caused him to jump, to grip the hilt of the sword he'd selected for Sophie. Another bone fell free, a vertebra that rolled rattling across the floor. And then, in an instant, all of the walls of bones around him collapsed in an explosion of bone and dust and mustiness.

Will jumped back towards the door and for the briefest moment he imagined it a stroke of luck that he would see the walls that these bones had concealed for so long. It lasted only as long as it took him to realise that the bones were not falling, they were moving, hurtling, a maelstrom punctuated by a hailstorm of clicks as bone found bone and locked together.

Within seconds, he could see the beginnings of the skeletons these had been forming out of the bone-storm, ribcages with skulls atop – *click, click* – an arm attached – *click, click, click* – fingers. Another second later, one of those reanimated arms lashed out at him. Will automatically hit back, sending the bones scattering again before they hurtled back to the skeleton they belonged to.

He reached for the door handle, just as he saw another skeletal hand emerge from the confusion, this time wielding one of the remaining swords. Will struck quickly, parrying the blow and lunging back into the confusion as bony limbs lashed out at him.

They pushed at him too, a wall of a dozen skeletons, barging, crashing and clattering, pushing a wedge between him and the door. He caught another glint as once more a sword was wielded at him with astonishing speed. He hit it away, all the time fending off sharp blows from skeletal arms and legs. He threw himself into the wall of skeletons that had blocked the door, hurling them aside, even as they lashed out at him. In the scrum, his hand found the door handle.

He didn't wait then, but pulled the door open and leapt through it, slamming it shut even as the bones, or massed skeletons as they now were, clattered and banged against it. He put his hand over the lock, trying to ignore the noise, concentrating instead on the mechanism, working it shut. He heard it click into place and finally turned away.

Eloise was standing there, staring at him in disbelief. "Is everything . . .?" The noise was still deafening behind him. "What . . .?"

"I don't know, but I suspect we have no time to search for explanations. As you said, the quicker we find Higson, the better it will be for all of us."

Will picked up his own sword and the two of them ran up the steps and through the chapel and only as they walked towards the doors did Eloise speak again.

"What attacked you in there?"

212

"The dead, who of course have one crucial advantage in any fight." She looked confused. "They have nothing to lose."

"The skeletons attacked you?"

"Yes, and foolishly I left them with two swords, but I hope the door will hold them, for a time at least, until we find Higson."

They stepped outside, but met Sophie who was coming the other way and had overheard Will's last comment.

"We've found him. No need to go to the new house." She pointed out into the gathering dark and said, "He's running around the park like a madman."

Will handed her the sword and started to walk.

"Thanks. What kept you?"

The question was addressed to Eloise as they walked after him, struggling to keep up with his determined pace.

"Will got held up. Sorry."

Will could see Higson now, not running around exactly, but nervously pacing a small section of ground in the middle of the park, halfway between the two houses. And he was not mad, but afraid. Again Will thought of encountering Sophie here, Sophie who'd been spooked up at the new house. He wondered if Higson too had encountered the shapeshifter.

That creature was nowhere to be seen, but as soon as he thought of it, he looked up into the air and had little choice but to stare in awe. Eloise and Sophie almost ran into him, but then they stopped too and looked up at the sky.

"What are we looking at?" asked Sophie. Then she saw and said, "Oh wow, what kind of birds are those – they look enormous."

They were higher than she realised, and bigger, but they were not birds – they were the winged devils Will and Eloise had seen in the cathedral and then perched on the school roof. There were not four of them now, but dozens, perhaps a hundred or more, circling gracefully across the vault of the night sky, waiting.

"They're not birds," said Eloise. "They're like devils."

"Then we're seriously outnumbered." Sophie sounded genuinely concerned, but her next comment managed to catch Will by surprise. "We need a plan, Will. We can't take them on out here in the open."

He looked at her, stunned by her courage and by that fierceness that was once more in her eyes. Eloise looked on, equally stunned, though Will suspected with less admiration.

"You might well be right, Sophie, but the creatures above are on our side."

"Oh, well that's jolly lucky."

A voice came out of the darkness. "Who's there?" It was Higson.

Will started walking again and was only a short distance away when he said, "I wish you no harm, Dr Higson!"

Higson backed away a couple of paces, but still appeared reluctant to make a run for the new house. Whatever he'd experienced there had scared him as much as Will did.

"You wish me nothing but harm!"

Will continued to walk towards him and said, "Wyndham isn't here to protect you, and there is nowhere to run from here that will offer you an escape. So I have no reason to lie."

"Then what do you want?"

"Lorcan Labraid."

"I don't know what you're talking about."

Will could see him clearly now, and could see that he was lying, that Wyndham had indeed found the way to reach the Suspended King.

"Wyndham took you through the gateway in the chapel storeroom. But no door is visible."

There was a moment of silence, only the gentle swishing of wings high above, and then Higson saw Will for the first time and looked at him as he said, "And if I tell you?"

Will laid his sword at his feet and said, "I give you my word, Dr Higson, that I will leave you unharmed. I wish only to go where my fate has been leading me all these long centuries."

Higson nodded to himself, but still didn't speak. He turned and looked towards the stand of trees that obscured the new house. Even now, even though his situation was hopeless, Wyndham still had enough of a hold on him that he was reluctant to talk.

Finally he faced Will again and said, "No doubt you took the key from my office drawer, but you took the wrong key."

"I don't understand," said Will, not bothering to remind Higson that he had no need for keys.

"There are two keys. One will open the storeroom door. The other opens the storeroom door and simultaneously releases the interior doors. If you don't use the correct key on the first door, you would never, in all your years of searching, know that there is a secret passage within that room."

That explained the hidden mechanism within the wooden panelling. He could only presume it explained the apparent lack of an opening in the stone wall too. Will wished he had time to go and find Harriet's spirit, to tell her even now how Henry had fooled them all, a master to the end.

And at the same time, Will wondered if Henry had known of the power Will's kind possessed over locks. If he had not known, then he'd accidentally chanced upon a method of ensuring no vampire would find that gateway.

"Thank you, Dr Higson, and I will keep my word, but I advise you not to . . ."

The ground shook. Will picked up his sword, though he doubted it would be needed, sensing the shapeshifter was about to reappear.

Higson looked around, panicked, and said, "What was that? It's coming back, isn't it? You have to protect me from it!"

So it *was* the shapeshifter he'd encountered.

"It won't harm you while I'm . . ."

Again Will stopped, as the ground started to tremble more and more violently beneath them. Higson looked down at his feet where the grass appeared to be pulsing and pushing up into a small mound. He staggered off it, looking at Will and at the ground with increasing alarm.

"You promised," he said feebly.

"This is not my doing," said Will, and he started to back away himself. Eloise and Sophie moved back with him, but they hadn't gone far when the tremor intensified and the ground ruptured and churned and something burst forth into the night.

Simultaneously, Will couldn't believe his eyes and yet

knew exactly what was happening here and who was responsible. Here in the park of Marland Abbey School, an ancient warrior had just charged out of the earth on a chariot, the chariot drawn by a horse, but both animal and rider nothing more than bones beneath their armour and tackle.

The rider brought his horse and chariot around in a tight, swift circle, and then instantly, too quickly for Will to even see it, he hurled a spear which cut through the darkness and struck Will in the centre of the chest, denting the armour, knocking him backwards.

The chariot swept past and Will swiped at the skeletal rider with his sword, scattering the bones from his right arm, which flew into the air, but then rebounded towards their owner as if drawn by some magnetism. Will knew that within seconds the warrior would turn and attempt a second strike.

The ground was shaking continually now too, and Will could see it pulsing across the entire park. There had been a great battle here in ancient times, and now Wyndham was reanimating the long-buried dead of that conflict to destroy Will.

He thought of what Wyndham had said about innocents being hurt and, turning to Sophie and Eloise, he said, "Get to the school, find the key. And wait for me there."

Sophie said, "But . . ." Will heard a whoosh and knocked another spear out of the air just in time. Several armoured foot soldiers had appeared a short distance away, and more were heaving themselves from the churning earth.

"Now! I need you to go now!"

Eloise grabbed hold of Sophie by the arm and started to pull her across the park. They screamed as the earth split in front of them and another chariot emerged, but the rider turned, moving round them as if they were nothing more than an obstacle, and careered towards Will. The other chariot had also turned and was heading back towards him.

He readied himself, but just as they were almost upon him he heard those distinctive wingbeats and two of the devils swooped down, plucking the warriors from their chariots and tearing away into the sky with them. The horses ran on blind with their chariots, passing Will and blasting through the ranks of the dead.

Will looked around the park, and in every direction now there was a chaos of skeletal warriors, on foot, on horseback, in chariots, and all of them were moving towards him. Nearby, Higson was spinning in circles, crying out, then he simply dropped to the ground and covered his head.

Will heard the familiar sound of spears and moved

219

quickly, avoiding the path of one, knocking another two aside, and then he ran towards the army of dead warriors, charging into them with his sword, with his fist, tearing them apart.

The devils that had filled the sky swooped continuously too, plucking away the warriors, smashing the skulls. He wondered at the shapeshifter's absence, but then as he fought the continuous onslaught, he saw first one, then another skeleton warrior being sucked back into the ground. It could only be the creature, though in what guise he didn't know.

Yet still the dead came, the entire moonlit landscape full of them, all of them pressing towards one point in the park, where Will was standing. What momentous battle could have been fought here that so many had perished?

For all the work of the devils and the shapeshifter, Will found himself fighting continuously on all fronts at once, aided only by the sword which seemed to sing in his hand, finding his enemies as if of its own volition, and by the armour given to him by Eloise.

Twice more he was struck by spears, once in the front, once in the back, the armour holding firm each time. Then in what felt like a momentary lull, Will sensed the air moving and turned to see a broadsword sweeping towards his neck, wielded by an armoured foot soldier who must have been a giant in his day.

Will raised his own sword just in time, blocking the blow, stopping the enemy blade just shy of his neck. He dropped to his knees then, sliding his sword free, striking two quick, fierce blows at his opponent. He was about to strike a third when the warrior was hoisted into the air by one of the marauding devils.

And in the gap opened by the warrior's disappearance, Will saw Sophie running back across the park, hacking with her sword at the attacking army, which still seemed unaware of her. He fought on, but kept glancing in her direction, and when she'd almost reached him, she shouted to him, "Eloise has got the key! She's waiting for us!"

"You should have stayed too."

But his words were lost, as she set about the approaching warriors, protecting one flank for him with a dazzling and determined display of fighting skills. There was no denying that she would be a queen to be reckoned with.

Will heard the telltale approach of chariots and turned to see three charging towards them, sometimes smashing through foot soldiers who were too slow to move in their own driven pursuit of Will. Immediately the devils swept down, heaving the warriors up into the sky.

Two of the runaway chariots clashed and flew into

the air. Even as Will fought off two soldiers, he shouted, "Sophie, watch out!"

She turned, skipping out of the way as one of the chariots crashed and gouged through the ground next to her. She looked at Will, laughing, manic, her eyes full of excitement, and then a shield spun through the air and struck her on the head. He was stunned to see her, even now, trying to ward off what she'd presumed was a warrior, wielding her sword, but then staggering. She looked at Will again, confused now, and slowly crumpled to the floor.

He felt anger seethe up inside him, and without realising what he was doing, he drove his sword into the ground and made to run to her. But no sooner had the tip of the sword pierced the earth than silence descended, no less than if time had been frozen.

Nothing moved. Had Will done this? Had his anger alone been enough, or was it something to do with the sword? Could it be that the act of driving this sword into the earth had been enough to undo Wyndham's magic? If so, no wonder the weapon sang in Will's hand.

The devils swooped over the battlefield, but seemed curious now at the stillness and silence, and then arced back up into the sky, resuming their earlier holding positions. The army of the dead stood motionless, completely robbed of the life that had briefly reanimated it.

Slowly, the ground began to churn again, but now the skeletons fell apart, clattering, tumbling into the mud, gradually being dragged back into the earth. Without thinking, Will pulled his sword free, then looked up to be sure that the act didn't reverse the process, but the park continued to cleanse itself in front of him.

He ran over to Sophie. She'd taken a fierce knock on the head, but she was still alive. He was relieved to see it had been a blunt impact too, that she wasn't bleeding. He took her sword and slipped both weapons through his belt before picking her up.

The park was quiet now, only a soft continuous squelching as the earth pulled everything back that was its own.

But then Will heard Higson, shrill behind him, crying out, "Oh, please, please leave me alone, I'll do whatever you ask . . ."

Will turned. Standing in a circle around the headmaster were a dozen identical versions of the shapeshifter boy, staring at him. Higson still gabbled on as one of the boys turned to Will and smiled. Will nodded and watched as the boy turned back to face Higson.

In an instant, they clicked and transformed into the monstrous insect, then suddenly into something serpent-like before melting away immediately into the ground. Higson looked astonished, staring across at Will, but within seconds his expression changed again to one of fear and panic.

"What's happening? You promised me!"

Will wasn't sure what Higson meant until he looked at the ground and saw that Higson appeared buried in it up to the ankles. And he was being pulled lower, up to his knees now, as if in quicksand.

"Help me! You have to pull me free! I'm being sucked in . . ." He let out a scream. "Don't just stand there, I'm being . . ." He was up to his waist now and put his arms on to the grass, trying desperately to stop his descent.

But Will did just stand there, holding the unconscious body of Sophie in his arms. He wasn't sure if he could save Higson anyway, nor did he know if the shapeshifter or some other force was dragging him into that subterranean world, but he sensed it was a fitting end for this man who had so spectacularly betrayed the trust of the children in his care.

Higson was screaming now as his shoulders disappeared into the ground. Then the screaming stopped, and finally his arms and hands disappeared, still tearing frantically at the grass.

In the silence that followed, Will heard a car engine behind him at the school. He turned and saw it speeding away from the building, spitting gravel behind it. Will stared with horror, and for a moment the world seemed to grow unsteady around him, almost as if he was about to pass out.

The battle had been intended to finish Will off, but he should always have expected Wyndham to have a back-up plan. And Will felt stupid and full of self-loathing because Wyndham had even hinted often enough as to what that plan would be.

Will started to run, and ran as fast as he could because it was Chris's car that was driving away. Will was desperate for there to be another explanation for what he could see, but he could think of only one. This had been Chris's role in the battle, to take the one thing from Will that he could not bear to go on without.

24

The barrow was completed in a few short months, and Lorcan Labraid was bound and suspended from its roof, the stake still in place through his heart. The witch used her magic to ensure that these bindings might never be loosened.

Labraid's magic also continued its work, ensuring that none could remove his head. It didn't deter those who would try. For many years after the great battle, someone hopeful of attaining the status of hero would visit the barrow on the full moon closest to that date and attempt this final act.

The result was always the same. The blade would strike the Suspended King's neck as if hitting rock, and shortly thereafter, the noble warrior's blood would leave his body all at once, a crimson vapour immediately absorbed by Lorcan Labraid, replenishing him, giving him ever greater vitality.

Everything else of these warriors crumbled into dust, everything except the sword, which would move of its own accord and lie on the floor beneath Labraid's head. Over the years, many swords were collected there and Labraid still did not perish.

A temple flourished at the site, but the witch was uneasy. It seemed to her that Lorcan Labraid had become the Grykken, attracting interest from afar, warriors seeking to emulate the brave exploits of those four ancient kings. These warriors could not even understand that this was one of the ancient kings before them, that Labraid should have been a lesson to them in their search for glory.

Her real fear though was that the fame of this sacred prisoner would one day attract someone with the power and the desire to overcome her magic and free him. The prophecies allowed for no such happening, but still the thought plagued her.

Nearing the end of her days, when she was one of the few still alive who could remember the events that had unfolded there, she performed her final act in the imprisonment of Lorcan Labraid. The days of magic were coming to an end, she was certain of that, but she used the last of hers to seal the two gateways to Labraid's burial chamber.

Mindful of the prophecies, and determined not to interfere with the transit of the heavens, she ensured within her spell that the gates could be opened again, but only by the one who was to come. A boy, a noble son with the bloodlines of the four – his touch alone would open these wicked portals.

She ordered the temple destroyed then, and instructed her daughter to move some miles away from there, to shun those who ruled these lands and have nothing more to do with this craft. So it was that over generations, the daughters of daughters and more beyond abandoned what had been their birthright until it was little more than a vaguely spoken memory.

The place that would become Marland was abandoned. Grass grew where once a temple had stood, then trees. Talk lived on in the peoples who lived nearby, of a great battle that had been fought there, of the darkness and evil that had once reigned there.

And some still chose it as a place to worship and sacrifice to their gods. So strong was this abandoned place in their thoughts, that when at first the Christian monks came, they encouraged the construction of a church there, and then an abbey. Foundations were laid, and in the process of their excavation, long-hidden steps were exposed.

It became the holy order's secret, guarded more jealously than all their treasures. Little did those monks know that it was predestined to be thus. Little did they know that deep below them, beyond that disturbing pagan labyrinth, was the evil of the world, living still, and now under their protection as he awaited the birth of the one who was to come, William of Mercia.

25

Will couldn't run fast enough, he knew that, but he didn't relent, even as the sound of the car disappeared out on to the open road. He saw the two teachers standing not far from the main door of the school, staring out towards him and the park beyond.

They appeared mesmerised and he suspected they'd been drawn by the disturbance and had just witnessed the moonlit battle. It was little wonder they were in shock. Nor did they seem to notice Will's approach until he was almost on them and then the younger one let out a small scream, which somehow brought them both out of their stupor.

"That car," shouted Will. "Who was in that car?"

The older teacher, Miss Bettencourt, turned and looked behind them and said, "I don't know. I didn't notice a car."

He ignored her and walked past them saying, "Help me. Sophie has been hurt."

"Of course," said Miss Bettencourt. "We'll . . . yes, inside."

There was a small sofa in the reception hall and Will laid Sophie on it.

The two teachers followed him in and the younger one stared at him now and said, "Who are you?"

"She may have some car keys about her person – look for them." Will walked off towards Higson's office, calling out Eloise's name. The office was empty, but looked ransacked, either in a struggle or in Eloise and Sophie's search for the key.

He marched back out and found the teachers tending to Sophie. As she saw him approach, the younger one stood and held up the car keys.

"Do you drive?" She nodded. "Good, then you come with me."

She shook her head, but couldn't speak, and then the older one said, "Should I call the police or . . . who should I call?"

Will fixed her eyes, catching her, and said, "You call no one. Look after Sophie and wait for us to return."

He didn't wait for a response, but walked back out into the night and there, where the tyres had scored tracks in the gravel, he saw a key. He walked over and picked it up. She'd dropped it there intentionally, he was sure of that, in the hope that he would not be hindered, even if she could not be with him.

Will looked at it, caring nothing for what it offered him right now, and he could only think of something Eloise had said – "Wyndham will target your heart." That he had done, but in a way that no armour could protect against. He heard a footstep behind him and turned to see the young teacher, mousy and serious and wide-eyed with fear.

"Where do you want to go?"

"I need to go where that car is going." He pointed into the night, where even now he could hear the faintest trace of the engine.

"And you know where that is?"

"No." Will looked back at the park and said to himself, "If only Higson was still here – he would know."

"Is Dr Higson dead?"

"I don't know, but I suspect wherever he is, he's unable to tell me where that car is headed."

"Maybe his satnav can." Will turned and looked at her, his stare so intense that she took a step back. "These are his keys, right? Well if he's been there before, it might be in his satnav."

He didn't have time to ask what a satnav was so he simply said, "Show me."

The teacher nodded nervously and led the way to the side of the school where Higson's car was parked.

She climbed into the driver's seat and Will walked to the other side, pulled the two swords free and climbed in. She was already looking at a small screen on the dashboard, so bright that it hurt Will's eyes.

"Will this place be local?"

"I imagine so."

"OK, 26 Mandela Crescent?" That didn't sound like a house where Wyndham would be found. Will shook his head. "Mapham Hall?"

"Where's that?"

"It's in the middle of nowhere, about five miles from here. In that direction." She pointed in the direction Chris's car had taken.

"You know the way?"

She smiled at him awkwardly, and seemed to understand now that he was not of this world because she nodded and said, "The machine will tell me."

She set off and as she drove her nerves lessened a little. She still kept her eyes on the road, but she said, "We haven't been formerly introduced. I'm Lucy Lawrence. I'm a teacher at the school."

"I'm Will."

"Hello, Will," she said, risking a glance across at him. "And you're the reason Eloise has been missing so much school this year?"

It seemed an odd thing to concentrate on, given that

she had just witnessed a battle involving devils and a dead army, and a shapeshifter that had apparently sucked her headmaster into the earth beneath the school.

"I am."

"Well, it's very irresponsible. She's fallen behind a great deal. And I know it's her fault too, but I can see how any young girl would fall under the spell of someone like you. So I think you should stop."

Will said, "You have no reason to be afraid of me."

"As it happens, I'd rather not think about that, just as I'd rather not think about anything that's happened this evening."

"I commend you for that. It's for the best."

She glanced quickly at him again, suspicious as she said, "How old are you? No boy of your age speaks like that."

"I thought you didn't want to think about it."

"You're right, I don't."

The machine instructed her to turn right, on to a narrow road. Will was confident now, certain that this matched the direction he'd heard Chris's car travelling in. It reminded him a little of the road to Puckhurst, but though Miss Lawrence peered at the road ahead, he expected no witches to appear in front of them this time.

She'd been silent for a short while, but cleared her

throat and said, "What are you going to do? When you get there?"

"I hope to rescue Eloise and return with you to the school."

"And what about the people who've taken her?"

"If she's harmed, I'll kill them."

"I didn't mean that, I . . . You'll kill them?"

"Of course, if they've harmed her."

"And if they haven't?"

"We'll find out soon enough – I see a gatehouse up ahead on the left."

She slowed the car as they approached. The lodge was in darkness. There were electric gates, but as the car turned in towards them, they slowly opened and Miss Lawrence drove through.

The gates had probably been set to open, perhaps for Chris's return. Will doubted very much that it signified a trap because Wyndham could never have expected Will to find him – his aim had been only to keep Eloise from his side. That in itself suggested how crucial Wyndham believed she was to the fulfilment of Will's destiny. But that in turn suggested Wyndham would think nothing of killing her.

They drove for some distance through dense woods before emerging into a park. Up ahead was a sprawling late-Gothic house. Lights were on here and there, but there was nothing inviting about it.

Miss Lawrence slowed and peered ahead. "Of course! I thought I recognised the name and couldn't think why." She turned to Will and seemed to have quite forgotten who he was and how she'd met him. "This used to be an insane asylum."

"How appropriate," said Will.

"Should I turn off the lights?"

"No," said Will. "If they don't know we're here already, they will soon."

He could see Chris's car parked in front of the house. There was another car too, a black limousine. As they approached, the main door opened and light spilled out. A young man in a suit came out and stood looking at their car.

Will put on his sunglasses, and said to Miss Lawrence, "Stop a little way before you reach the other car. And wait for us. Promise me you'll do that."

She nodded.

"Good. I'll leave this sword in the car, though I doubt you'll need it."

"What? No! You're not leaving a sword in my car."

She sounded oddly determined, something Will couldn't help but find amusing.

"It's not your car."

"That's not the point. I'm . . . *in loco parentis*, or

236

whatever it is you are with a car. I do not want you to leave weaponry in here. What if I'm attacked and the attacker gets hold of the sword?"

She was pulling to a stop so he said, "As you wish, I'll take it, but trust me, you are unlikely to be attacked."

Miss Lawrence stopped the car and said, "Good. Thank you."

Will opened the door and as he got out he slipped the spare sword into his belt and studied the illuminated face of the man who awaited him.

26

"This is private property – please drive back to the road immediately."

Will reasoned that the man couldn't see him while he was still behind the headlights. He was young, too young to be Wyndham. Will closed the car door and walked towards him.

"I said this is . . ." He saw Will's face now and after registering surprise, he spoke urgently into some sort of radio attached to his collar. "He's here, Mr Wyndham, he's . . ."

Will hit him hard with the back of his hand, knocking him off his feet and sending him tumbling across the ground. Will looked, fearing he'd misjudged the power with which he'd struck him, but the man was merely unconscious.

Will turned back to the house, but all the lights were extinguished at once. A moment later, they were replaced with a sickly light that appeared to seep through the interior. Will guessed it was some sort of emergency lighting, but it also resembled the odd light that had filled the new house when Wyndham had summoned the spirits.

He didn't hesitate and moved quickly inside, stopping in the hallway only to listen. In that moment he could see that Wyndham had done little to turn this place into a home. It looked as if nothing very much had been done to it since its last days as an asylum. There was even the faint smell of sickness and medicine and disinfectant about it.

Will looked around, but couldn't see where the light was coming from. And now he wondered if Wyndham *had* performed his same conjuring trick with the spirits of this place as he had at the new house because there was noise rising up everywhere, a murmuring of many voices, echoing quietly but persistently through the building.

He heard a cry then that he recognised immediately and a moment later she called his name. Will ran up the stairs and stopped to listen. He heard his name called again, but was less certain this time that it was Eloise, and then it was called a third time, but from a different direction.

It had seemed to come from the floor above to the left, but now it was on the same floor as him and to the right. And still there was the constant thrum of other

239

voices, some laughter somewhere along one of those long corridors, a door creaking as if in a breeze.

He stayed on this floor and took the corridor to the right. Many of the rooms still had the doors that had been designed to keep the unfortunate inmates secure, most of them closed. But just before a turn in the corridor he found a room with a door ajar.

He stopped and looked inside. An old man in a long white smock was sitting on the edge of a bed, rocking back and forth, gently mumbling to himself. He became aware of Will standing there and turned to look up at him, a hopeless expression on his troubled face. He didn't stir further than that, but turned his face forward again and continued to rock.

Will had almost admired Wyndham for the way he'd summoned up the spirits of the dead in the new house. But there was something unforgivable about bringing back these tortured souls into a life that had treated them so harshly.

Will continued on his way. The disembodied cries and whimpers were louder up ahead and as he turned another corner, he found the cries of anguish, the manic voices, the shouts of despair becoming overwhelming. Turning another corner, he saw the spirit of a creature that looked barely human, scurrying along the corridor ahead of him and into a room.

He noticed then that he was passing a heavy steel door which was open now, but designed to seal the corridor. Given the volume of the disturbed noises coming from the spirits in the rooms ahead, Will imagined this had been the section of the asylum once set aside for the most troubled and dangerous patients.

Yet even above the din, he heard his name called once again, up ahead, and this time it was recognisably Eloise. He increased his speed, but stopped again and took a few steps back, examining the metal frame of the door, the heavy bolts that supplemented the lock.

Somehow, it looked newer than the rest of the fittings. Was this a trap of some sort? Will looked around, to make sure Wyndham had not fitted cameras here about, but he couldn't see any. He had to ensure this door could not be closed, locking him within one section of the building.

He put his hands into his pockets, felt the journals still inside. Then his fingers found the knife. He took it out. So recently it had seemed inappropriate to use this knife for anything else, but as he stared at it, he sensed inexplicably that he would never use it again to take blood. He crouched down and jammed the point of the blade deep into the floor between the hinge of the open door and the frame. If Wyndham tried to close this door now, he'd find it obstructed and would not know why.

Will walked on.

"Will!" He picked up his pace, turned another corner, and then the corridor seemed to shudder as a loud bang sounded behind him. The spirits momentarily fell silent and then set off again, worse than before.

Will was disappointed that Wyndham had not been more imaginative, but then he supposed the sorcerer had never really expected Will to come here. And besides, until three weeks ago his main residence had been elsewhere – he'd had little time to adapt.

Will turned and ran back along the corridor. The door banged again, reverberating violently as it clashed against the small but effective obstacle of the knife. It banged a third time as Will turned the corner which brought it back into view and there he saw Chris as the door bounced back again.

Chris saw him too and let out a panicked cry and sprinted away along the corridor. Will ran after him, and even with Chris's head start he was surprised to turn a corridor ahead and find no trace of Chris hurrying away. He slowed, taking in the air, his senses confused slightly by the overpowering medicated odour of the place.

Will reached the open door and turned to see the old man, rocking gently still. He glanced at Will and smiled a little, a smile so pitiful that even if this was but a shadow, Will wished desperately that there was something he could do for him.

"It's time for you to come out, Chris, to face the truth of what you've done."

There was no response, but then the old man looked into the corner of his room, beyond the door, as if waiting to hear what Chris would say. Will stepped into the room, his sword at the ready, and turned to face the corner.

Chris was standing there, one hand partially shielding his eyes, no doubt for fear of being mesmerised, the other pointing a weapon of some sort at Will's chest. It looked to Will like a cross between a pistol and a crossbow, and the metal bolt sitting within it appeared dangerously similar to the one that had disabled him so recently. He wondered if it would be powerful enough to pierce the armour he was wearing. It hardly mattered because Chris's hand was trembling so violently that he was more likely to hit Will's heart by accident than by design.

Will should have felt nothing but hatred for Chris, who had betrayed him more with this final act, the abduction of Eloise, than even Will could have imagined. He did not feel hatred, though. From the corner of his eye, Will could still see the very real spirit of the old man, rocking and mumbling, and yet it was Chris who looked the more pitiable.

He looked like a ruined man, drawn and sleepless with dark patches around his eyes. Just a few months before, seeing him in The Whole Earth, Chris had looked so healthy, so youthful, and only now did Will realise that the glow of well-being had slowly been fading from him. He looked a shadow of his former self, as much a spirit as those conjured by Wyndham within these halls.

"Where is he, Chris, and what does he plan to do with Eloise?"

"Don't move any closer!" His hand trembled more violently, but then, seeing perhaps that Will wasn't moving, he said, "He's keeping her from you, that's all, stopping you from ruining her life."

Will didn't think Chris really believed that, didn't think Chris was even sure of what he was doing here.

"Chris, you think I betrayed you at Puckhurst. I didn't. I bargained with Asmund only to secure Eloise's release. I would have fought for you."

Chris was shaking his head and said, "He said all along you would, and then you did, and I felt such a fool, standing there, trapped, knowing Wyndham had been right."

And there it was, proof that Chris had been in league with Wyndham even before Puckhurst.

Will laughed and said, "You foolish young man. Twenty years ago you filmed me, an act which you said

244

had shaped your life, and yet still you were so quick and so willing to betray me. And why? Is it because, in truth, you have been afraid for twenty years, afraid of this moment?"

Chris fired. The bolt burst through the armour, knocking Will back a step. There was the answer to that question at least. The armour had slowed the bolt and the end of it still stuck out, but enough had gone in to pierce the heart – had it been on target.

Will could feel the bolt in his flesh just below his ribs. He reached down and pulled it free, but as he did so, Chris made a desperate attempt to run past him and out of the door. He slipped, and though he only brushed against the edge of Will's sword, he stumbled into the door frame, clutching his side.

Will looked down at him, surprised that so slight a contact could have injured him. Yet it had, and the blood seeped through Chris's shirt, the rich scent of it catching in Will's nostrils, reawakening a hunger he still hoped might be weeks away. Chris looked down at the wound himself, crying, perhaps with the realisation of what would surely follow.

"Please, I only . . . I would never . . ."

"Where is he?"

He looked up at Will and pointed to the floor above.

"I'm begging you, Will, I . . ."

"Leave now, Chris. Leave this place now. I will not spare you again."

Chris looked up in shock, climbing back to his feet, and as if the foundations of his world had just shifted, he could say only, "Why?"

The scent of blood was overpowering, the sight of it, slick and sticky on Chris's fingers, even more tempting.

"Because as much as you would wish me to be, I am not a monster. Now go."

Chris tried to run away, but yelped a little in pain and slowed to a messy stumbling gait. Will turned briefly and looked at the spirit of the old man, still rocking, oblivious again.

Before he left the room, Will took the journals from his pockets and stuffed them up under the armour, positioning them above his heart. If Wyndham had a similar weapon, Will had no doubt he'd wield it with more accuracy than Chris. There was something fitting too in having Harriet's words as protection.

And with that, he followed the spattered blood trail, through the wails and moans of those corridors, out to the main staircase where he climbed another floor. A corridor stretched out in one direction, closed double wooden doors in the other.

"Wyndham!"

Almost immediately a reply came from beyond the

double wooden doors, Eloise shouting, "Will, don't! Don't come in!"

There was no attempt to silence her. And in that at least Wyndham knew him well enough, and knew that nothing would stop Will going through those doors.

27

He didn't reach for the handle, and didn't bother to stop and judge if Wyndham had electricity running through it. He simply kicked the middle of the double doors, which burst open with such force that one broke from its hinges and crashed to the floor. There were sparks too, so Will had been right about the electricity.

The doors opened on to a long room, stretching along that entire half of the building. It was panelled on one side, windowed along the other. Had it been constructed as a long gallery? Or some sort of recreation room? Either way, the room was empty now, except for the two people standing at the far end.

One was Wyndham, immediately recognisable with his dark suit and short grey hair. He was standing behind Eloise, a knife held to her throat. In his other hand, he held a gun at his side, similar to the one Chris had used, but Will could see from here that Wyndham's held more than one bolt. Eloise, for her part, was standing motionless, her feet bound with rope, her hands tied in front of her.

Eloise shouted, "Will, get out! I dropped the key at the school. You can go through on your own."

"Quiet now," said Wyndham. "He knows that will not do."

"I am not leaving," said Will.

Wyndham smiled.

Will walked forward carefully, checking the room for hidden traps, though he could see none. He heard a car start outside and pull away, Chris's car. Wyndham raised his arm, but Will kept walking. When he was halfway along the room, Wyndham fired, the bolt glinting in the strange light as it hurtled through the air.

Eloise screamed at the same time as the bolt hit Will directly over the heart, stopping him, forcing him to take a backwards step. He looked down. The bolt had punched easily through the armour, and he could feel too that it had powered through the two journals and punctured his skin, but no more than that.

Will smiled as he pulled the bolt free and said, "You should read the prophecies more closely – as of the full moon, I am immune to such things."

Doubt crossed Wyndham's face for a moment, but then he himself smiled and said, "Then remove your armour."

"Remove yours."

Wyndham looked at Eloise, then back at Will as he said, "I think not. You see, I *have* read the prophecies. I'll kill her before allowing you your evil destiny."

"If you kill her, I will kill you."

"It doesn't matter. My work will be done. I have lived too long anyway."

Chris had looked steadily more drained, but the opposite could be said for Wyndham. It was true, Will had seen only a moving image of him before, but in the flesh he looked strong and powerful, despite the grey hair. It was almost as if Wyndham was the vampire, drawing energy and power from those around him. And all that energy was redirected towards the destruction of Will.

"Why do you persist, Mr Wyndham, in your belief that I am evil? Will you not tell me the reason why you have so hated me these past centuries?"

At first he thought Wyndham would not answer, but then he said, "Very well, as at least one of us will not leave this room alive, I will grant you that. I was born, like you, into a life of great privilege. 1734, the youngest son of the fourth Lord Bowcastle. My mother, before her marriage, was Miss Arabella Harriman."

Will did not move, but he felt as if another bolt had struck him in the chest. No armour and no journals

250

could protect him from the shock of hearing that name.

"I see the name is familiar to you, as it should be, given that you haunted her through her youth. And then pursued her again, even as a mature woman. You may not remember the night, but you appeared beside her coach, permanently unsettling her well-being, and in that act you set me on this path. What is a child to do when his mother has been the victim of evil."

"Not of evil, Mr Wyndham, but of love. And I believe she felt the same way about those youthful encounters."

"Nonsense!" His anger was so sudden that he pressed the knife harder against Eloise's throat. She pulled her head back, trying to escape the blade. He calmed then.

"No, Mr Wyndham, there was nothing to it, a chaste and innocent friendship across several summers, but it was powered by love, not evil. And I do remember that night years later, I remember the look of horror on her face, and how I wished myself dead."

"You didn't wish hard enough," said Wyndham coldly.

"True," said Will. "I thank you anyway, for finally telling me the root of your hatred. And now I ask you to let the girl go. You know that killing her will not stop me. The prophecies speak of two queens, a choice to be made, and the other is still unharmed at the school."

"Is she?" Wyndham laughed. "Are you talking about the wonderfully impressionable Sophia Hamilton? And she looks just right, doesn't she?"

Even as Will had spoken, he'd wondered at this. Wyndham had known about Sophie, had written to her, and he had known about the prophecies. So why would he put so much store in ending Will's flight to destiny by killing Eloise alone? Eloise had suggested the explanation herself.

"Imogen," said Wyndham. He laughed again now, at Will's confused expression, and said, "I fooled you all, even the spirits. I suspect even Lorcan Labraid knows no better."

"Who is Imogen? What do you speak of?"

"Oh I had a long time to prepare for this, half a century from the time I discovered it. Two children born, both with a destiny, that William of Mercia would choose between them for his queen. Lucky them." He looked full of contempt, for Will, for Eloise, for all those who were set against him. "I couldn't allow it of course. Imogen and her parents were killed in a car accident. Eloise should have met with the same fate, but she survived her family's catastrophe."

Eloise's face drained of colour. For a moment Will wondered if she might faint at the revelation, but she didn't, and her emotions solidified into a steely anger.

"I tried several times more, but each time it was as if some other force was protecting her. I know not why. Finally I realised it might be in my interest to keep her alive. Your destiny would lead you to her, and that in turn would lead you to me."

"You killed my family?"

He looked at her and said, "It was regrettable, just as it was with the other girl, but it's a common thread through history that innocent people must sometimes die in the cause of a greater good." He looked back to Will and said, "So you see . . ."

But he was cut short. Will had seen the anger and determination building up in Eloise's face and was dreading that she would act unwisely, but he couldn't have envisaged the speed and strength with which she moved.

She raised her hands, slipping the rope that bound them around the point of the knife, pulling it away from her throat as she spun away from Wyndham. At the same time she pushed him backwards and then completed her rotation and rolled towards the side of the room, shuffling clear.

Wyndham steadied himself quickly and took aim with his gun. Will pulled the sword from his belt and hurled it at full force at Wyndham. He hadn't given himself time to aim it or even consider his action, but the blade was true and the sword smashed into the gun and sent it flying across the room.

Wyndham was unharmed, but stood looking at his own hand as if he couldn't understand where the sword had come from or where the gun had gone. He ran towards the two fallen weapons then, dropping the knife and picking up both gun and sword, but by the time he turned, Eloise was behind Will. She'd pulled the frayed rope from her hands and Will could hear her working to untie the rope around her feet.

Wyndham nodded to himself, shocked by the turn of events, disappointed, and said, "I won't let you leave."

"I am not yet ready to leave. You have told me who you are, so now let me remind you, I am William, Earl of Mercia, and you have wronged me and my family and the people I love. You could so easily have been a good man, but you have taken that goodness and twisted it beyond recognition. But enough of what has been done – your time of reckoning is at hand."

"Very well. Will you make it fair?"

"Of course. Throw down your gun and I will remove my armour."

Wyndham tossed the gun aside. Will took off his coat and handed it to Eloise, then loosened the armour. The journals fell to the floor and Wyndham allowed himself a smile. Will took the armour off then, but as he placed it on the floor, Wyndham charged towards him, surprisingly fast. Will fended off a blow, then pushed him back, sword striking against sword, blow for blow. Wyndham was a skilled fencer, but once again Will found the sword in his own hand moving serenely through the air, almost without direction from him.

Wyndham tried another gambit. As Will drove him back again, he spotted his knife on the floor and swooped down to pick it up with his free hand. He countered then, charging at Will, striking blade against blade and then pushing the knife towards Will's chest.

Will moved quickly, too quickly for Wyndham, and in overextending himself, Wyndham had left himself exposed. Will's sword danced through the gap, slicing across the front of Wyndham's chest, cutting more deeply into his arm.

Wyndham dropped the sword and the knife and staggered backwards clutching his arm. The blood was pumping out of it. He appeared reluctant to raise his eyes, but did finally and smiled ruefully, realising that he was no match, that he had lost.

"Are you satisfied, sir?"

Even injured, he didn't look like an old man. Will thought of all that Wyndham had done, to Eloise and her family, to Marcus, to all those innocents he'd claimed so much to care for.

Oddly though, Will found himself dwelling most on noble Edgar, the vampire who'd begged Will to kill him after his long incarceration at Wyndham's hands. Yes, Edgar had been a vampire, had no doubt killed to survive, and yet in the end he had, it seemed to Will, possessed more humanity than this man who saw himself as the champion of good.

"No, Mr Wyndham, I am not satisfied."

Wyndham nodded, and looked to the side of the room. Will thought he might make another attempt to get the gun, now that Will had removed his armour, and he was ready for it. Sure enough, Wyndham ran, but just as Will prepared to throw his sword, Wyndham changed course. And with no more ceremony, he threw himself through the window, the glass shattering as his body flew out into the night.

Will and Eloise both ran to the window and looked down. In the moonlight, the shape of Wyndham's lifeless body was clearly visible on the gravel below.

They were silent for a short while, and then Eloise said, "Why did he do that, I wonder?"

"To deny us the satisfaction."

"What satisfaction could there be? I can never know my family."

"No." Will looked again at the body. "What a wasted life. What a waste of so much knowledge and wisdom and opportunity." He turned back to Eloise. "I'm sorry, how are you?"

She laughed. "I'm fine, and I'm sorry, I was so stupid to let Chris take me. I tried to get away from him, but . . ."

He shook his head and held her, and as they stood there he realised the building was once again at peace, and illuminated only by the moonlight. Everything of Wyndham's had died with him, and now there was no one else to blame, nothing more between Will and his destiny.

And Will realised it all came down to which of these two people was right. The man lying dead on the gravel below had believed him pure evil. The girl in his arms believed in his goodness. Only one of them could be right, and Will himself could only bear for it to be Eloise.

28

*M*y tale is almost told. My audience has travelled with me through this dark night, little knowing who it is who speaks to them, or that my own legend is yet to be written. And where are the holy men, the witches or shamans who will carry my story through the troubling times to come?

Where are those who will play their part as the monks at Marland did? For they studied their treasure well, exploring the labyrinth, deciphering prophecies in languages that were still not entirely lost. They were mindful too that the rulers of those lands would offer a protecting hand if they believed the abbey had a part to play in their own future glory.

The British kings who had ruled there had known something of the place's magical power. But the monks found the Anglo-Saxons who followed, and the Normans who followed them, were eager to play a part, even to the point of taking their wives from the noble lines of their predecessors, ensuring a greater connection with this place.

The witch had worked her magic well, and the monks never discovered the true secret of the labyrinth. Nor did they ever understand that Lorcan Labraid was not a spirit being, but a living king whose influence even now could be felt throughout those lands.

Witchcraft still continued, though well hidden, but the monks were always eager to steer their overlords away from such evil practices. Had the third Earl of Mercia ignored that advice, had he known of the wisdom that lay so close at hand, one of the greater tragedies of this history might have been avoided.

In the year 1240, the Earl's first child was expected. A woman was engaged to assist in the birth, a woman to whom the Countess became greatly attached. This midwife was of an illustrious line herself, and knew that this child was destined for greatness. She knew also, with the power of foresight she possessed, that the good Countess would be rendered infertile by the birth, and no more children would be born to her.

The Abbott had also come to a similar conclusion as to the importance of this child, based on genealogies rather than prophecy. He did not know, however, that the child's mother would produce no more offspring.

What was to be done? This child was the one of whom it had been spoken, but there could be no other to rival his claim.

The Abbott poisoned the Earl against the midwife and had her cast out. Two nuns, recommended by the Abbott himself, were brought in to assist in what was certain to be a difficult birth. And in that way, the Abbott of Marland arranged the murder of William of Mercia's mother. That man of God had done his work, knowing not what he did, what he had set in motion, nor who would oversee the remainder of the prophecy.

It was the Queen Elfleda, and those who did her bidding, who now took William in their charge. Asmund struck him down. They prepared his chambers, cleared a way for him as no mortal could have done. And so it continued through the following centuries. When William of Mercia plunged a stake into his own heart, it was Asmund who came into the city to remove it. Only when the sorcerer Wyndham started his work did they struggle, but still their faith in the prophecy was unwavering.

The day would come, there was no question of it, when William of Mercia would stare into Lorcan Labraid's eyes, just as the Suspended King had once stared into the eyes of the Grykken. William of Mercia, and he alone, would release Labraid from his mortal chains, severing his neck, sending him home, and in so doing they would become as one, and evil would reign.

29

How long had they been standing there in each other's arms? A minute perhaps? Time had been lost to them. But suddenly he felt a shudder of cold run through her and at the same time Will sensed they were not alone. He looked across the room and the spirits seemed to emerge out of the wood panelling.

The witches had promised only one more visit and he felt a certain sense of dread with the realisation that this was it. They stood in silence, so odd in itself that Will counted to check all seven were there.

"Why do you not speak?"

At first it seemed there would still be no response, but then the seventh said, "There is nothing more to say."

"Then why have you appeared before us?"

"Only to bid you farewell, William of Mercia."

"Farewell?"

"Make haste, or what has been opened will be closed again."

Will tried to speak, but all at once the seven witches

burst into flames, which dazzled brightly and then instantly died away, leaving nothing behind.

"They er . . ." said Eloise, but found no end to her sentence. She turned to Will and said, "How are we going to get back to school? Actually, how did you get here?"

"Miss Lawrence brought me in Higson's car."

"Miss Lawrence! Did you hypnotise her?"

Will shook his head. "She witnessed a battle between dead warriors and devils, and probably saw Higson being sucked into the earth by the shapeshifter. Come."

He took her by the arm and they started to walk as Eloise said, "Higson's dead?"

"He's underground. Whether he's dead or not, I cannot say. I don't know how the shapeshifter . . ."

"Best not think about it," said Eloise. "I'm still not sure how I'll be able to face Miss Lawrence normally on Monday morning."

They'd reached the stairs and descended quickly.

Will said, "I repeat, given what she has seen this evening, I don't think that should be a concern. Besides, are you confident there will be a Monday morning? We have not understood the prophecies yet, but does anything we've seen suggest the world will continue on its serene course after this evening, that the sun will rise in a blue sky, that the world will be at peace? I would wish it could be so, but I think not."

Eloise didn't answer and Will found himself thinking of his dreams, of Eloise among the ruins on a summer's day, of the warmth of her, but it was too much a dream, and more distant now than it ever was.

"They didn't bid me farewell. The witches."

"No."

"Doesn't that worry you?"

He looked at her and smiled. "No."

"Oh, OK." And then as they stepped outside, she said, "I dropped the key near Chris's car . . ."

"Yes, I have it, thank you."

"Good, so there's nothing stopping us."

Miss Lawrence saw them and started the car.

Will had detected some reluctance in Eloise's voice and he said, "There is nothing stopping us, but prophecies and destiny and witches be damned – I would not wish you to go through with this, whatever this is, if you do not wish to do so."

"Are you still going through with it?"

"I must."

"Then so must I. Whatever it is, I would rather go through it with you than avoid it without you."

He opened the door and said, "Miss Lawrence, I believe you know Eloise."

Miss Lawrence pointed, saying, "A man just crashed

264

through one of the windows. His body's over there. And another man came out bleeding. He drove off in a Range Rover."

Will looked across at Wyndham's body. "What happened to the other man, the one who came out to meet us?"

"Oh, he ran away. He ran in that direction. He looked really wobbly though."

Will got into the back with Eloise and said, "Thank you, Miss Lawrence, if you wouldn't mind taking us back to the school."

"Of course, what a splendid idea."

Eloise pulled a slightly concerned face at Will, then said, "Are you OK, Miss Lawrence?"

"Thank you for asking, Eloise, but I'm just fine, really I am. Now, I don't think we need the satnav to get back. Quite straightforward, wasn't it, Will?" She turned the car in a large circle before starting back down the drive and saying too casually, "You know, Eloise, this used to be an insane asylum."

"Yes. Yes, I knew that." Eloise looked at Will and whispered, "I think she's in shock."

Will nodded, finding the possibility less than surprising.

They sat in silence for a while, watching the headlights find a way for them along the rest of the drive and out into the lane. Will thought of what Wyndham had told him about the other girl, pitying Sophie for being so badly used, pitying the unknown Imogen and her family even more.

He thought of the picture on the wall of the chapel storeroom, and wondered if Imogen, killed when he was hibernating deep beneath the city walls, had carried the line. That would explain how he might have reigned alongside her.

"What are you thinking?"

He looked at her and said, "I was just thinking about the things Wyndham told us."

"You mean about his mother?" Oddly, Will had thought no more of that, perhaps because the Wyndham they'd encountered had seemed far too distant from the Arabella Will had known to really be her son, though he didn't doubt it.

"No, actually I was thinking about Imogen, whoever she was."

"I was thinking about her too. I wonder what she'd have been like, if we'd have been friends."

Will smiled and said, "You didn't care for Sophie much before you met her, and she wasn't even a real rival." And as he said it, he realised Wyndham hadn't fooled everyone – the shapeshifter had recognised Sophie as an impostor from the start, and had taken against her accordingly.

"True."

He looked at her then, and took her hand in his as he said, "I think I would have picked you anyway."

She squeezed his hand but said, "You probably say that to all your potential queens of the underworld."

Will laughed, but stopped as Miss Lawrence said, "Oh my goodness, what's gone on here?"

They looked forward and saw a car tipped into a ditch, the back end sticking up into the air. It was immediately obvious that it was Chris's car. There was still room to pass and Miss Lawrence drove just beyond the crashed vehicle before stopping.

Will got out and walked over, looking inside the wreckage. It looked as if Chris had left the road at some speed. Whether blood loss or the accident had been the end of him it was impossible to say.

Will got back into the car. "He's dead."

Miss Lawrence looked over her shoulder and said, "Are you sure? He might be . . ."

"Miss Lawrence, trust me, if Will says he's dead, he's dead."

"There's nothing we can do," said Will. "Please, drive on."

She looked him in the eyes, and even without Will attempting to mesmerise her, she appeared to understand, and a calm descended over her. She turned forward again and accelerated.

Eloise said quietly, "What will she do now?"

He knew she was talking about Rachel, her voice full of empathy for someone who would now be both betrayed and bereaved, her life shattered. Will didn't answer because there was no answer to give, and because they themselves didn't know what yet lay ahead of them.

When they reached the school, all was at peace. Miss Bettencourt came out at the sound of the car and as they got out she approached Miss Lawrence.

"Sophie's fine, but she'll have a bad head. I thought of calling the doctor, but the phones are out. I couldn't even work my mobile." She saw Will and hesitated, then spotted Eloise, and said, "Eloise, are you . . ."

Will said, "You should both go to Sophie and stay with her. There is something Eloise and I must do."

Miss Bettencourt said, "But . . ."

Miss Lawrence interrupted her. "Miriam, under the circumstances, I think it best we just . . . yes, we just . . . let's go and see Sophie. You know, any child with concussion should be kept under observation."

She ushered her older colleague away, but they had not gone far when Will said, "Miss Lawrence?" They both turned and he said, "Thank you, for everything."

She smiled, a smile that was teetering on the brink,

and the two teachers walked on into the school.

Will turned to Eloise. "You will need your torch."

She nodded, but then said, "No, better than that, I noticed a camping lantern in Higson's office. Go to the chapel and I'll meet you there."

Will smiled. "I've let you out of my sight once too often already."

So they went together to Higson's office and got the camping lantern, then made their way into the chapel and to the storeroom door.

Will took the key from his pocket and said, "Ready?"

"Ready."

He put the key in the lock, and turned it.

30

He could hear the mechanism make an extra turn, setting off something further within the wall, but nothing momentous. He opened the door and Eloise turned on her lantern. With a moment of panic, he expected her to see the picture he'd exposed of her, a skull in one hand, a sword in the other, but there was a plain wall in its place, a wall with a door set into it.

They both walked towards the wall and Will looked at it with wonder, at how precisely it had been built, and the skill that must have been employed to make it work so seamlessly.

"The wall that was here before, the additional lock must have caused it to slide up or down. This wall before had no door and was painted."

"With a picture of me," said Eloise, who held her lantern up to look once more at the picture of Will and a girl they now knew to be called Imogen, a girl killed in infancy because of her very portrayal on that wall.

Then she saw the picture on the end wall, of Will

sitting alone on a throne, atop a hill of mutilation and suffering. Will couldn't see Eloise's face, but he could see that she looked at it with horror. For a moment he feared it reminded her of the visions Wyndham had made her see in the labyrinth. But Wyndham was dead, and perhaps his power to influence had died with him.

Eloise shook her head and turned as she said, "No, this isn't you. It could never be."

Instinctively, Will reached up and held the half of broken pendant hanging from his neck. Eloise did the same with her half, and smiled. They had nothing more than that, the belief that they had not been brought together, had not waited seven hundred years, for such an ill-starred future.

Will turned to the door and opened it. There were steps on the other side and they descended together before reaching a passageway. It was reminiscent in so many ways of the entrance to the labyrinth. The passageway continued for some distance, and finally delivered them into a small circular chamber.

"Dead end," said Eloise. "That can't be right."

Will looked around the walls, the ceiling, the floor, and said, "As unpromising as it looks, I suspect this is the second gateway." Eloise looked sceptical and he added, "Remember, the circular chamber in the labyrinth was not obviously possessed of a gateway – it

271

was only seeing the portcullis design in the maze that told us it was there."

"Yes, that's true. So . . ." It was clear she still had no idea what to suggest.

Will pointed at the floor and said, "When Fairburn's ghost summoned all those spirits before me, my mother descended into the floor of the chamber, walking a circle around Fairburn just as if descending a spiral stone staircase."

"Good, so we need to open the floor."

Will smiled and said, "Have you any suggestions for how we might achieve that?"

"Will, for all these hundreds of years you've had power over locks." She shrugged. "Would it hurt to try?"

The simplicity of it caught him off guard, but he moved to the middle of the chamber, crouched down and placed his hand flat on the floor. Almost immediately he felt a stirring beneath his fingers, the ground trembling then shaking.

Eloise moved to the edge of the chamber. Will lifted his hand and stood back too, as the movement of stone continued beneath his feet, then as the ground began to shimmer and shift. And then it peeled apart, revealing a spiral stone staircase, exactly as Will had imagined it, descending into the darkness.

A smell rose up to them, a faint but unmistakable

smell of sulphur. Will descended first and Eloise followed. He stopped and waited for her at the bottom, another passageway stretching ahead. There were no paintings on these walls, but then Will suspected few mortal men would have spent time here, and fewer still would have chosen to stay and paint.

They started to walk and after a short distance the smell grew stronger, and Will could see the entrances to other tunnels up ahead. If this was the beginning of another labyrinth, he feared they would never find Lorcan Labraid.

But the decision on which way to go was taken for them. As they reached the junction, Eloise's lantern flickered across the other tunnels, which were packed as far as they could see with the devils that had so assisted them, roosting like bats, clinging to walls and ceiling in hunched shapes, all passive, eyes closed.

They walked on and Will said quietly, "It would appear that those who assisted me in battle were but a small advance party."

"You think these are all waiting to be released?"

"I suspect they're waiting to serve, in whichever capacity they're required."

This was a labyrinth, but at each fork or turn or junction, they found only one route left free for them. And only after some time did the choices diminish, until finally they were walking up a long single passage, a gentle incline. Quite unexpectedly, it opened up before them and they found themselves in a large circular chamber, a domed roof above them, the entrances to two further passages across on the other side.

But there, in the middle, suspended from the roof, was the saddest, most disturbing, most astonishing thing that Will had ever seen. He looked strong and still youthful, his black hair abundant, hanging down, his body powerful and muscled beneath the leather clothes.

Yet he was bound, and a stake was driven through his heart. Will knew how weakened he had to be, how impossible it would be for him to save himself while imprisoned in that fashion. And he thought of the agonies endured by this man over such vast tracts of time.

Eloise looked just as stunned and mesmerised by the sight, and all she could do was place her lantern on the floor and stand, watching. As outlandish a sight as it was, Will was certain that Eloise sensed exactly what he did, that this was a king before them.

It was more than that too, for whether or not Will would have chosen it for himself, this man's blood had once run through Will's veins, no less than his own father's had.

Perhaps that was one of the many emotions that

drove Will now, for without knowing quite what he was doing, he stepped forward, dropped to one knee before him, and said, "My Lord."

Lorcan Labraid opened his eyes, deep dark eyes. He smiled, revealing his fangs.

"So you have come at last. Welcome, noble prince." His eyes skipped across the room towards Eloise, but came back quickly to Will as he said, "And I see you chose my sword for your own – I trust it has served you well."

Will stood again, looking at the sword in his hand. Had he been subconsciously drawn to that sword and was this the reason he'd wielded it with such ease? Was this the reason Will had been able to overpower Wyndham's magic, simply by driving Lorcan Labraid's sword into the battlefield?

"It has served me well." He looked up at the bindings with which Labraid was attached to the roof and said, "It will serve me better if I use it to free you."

"Patience, young Will." Labraid's eyes were glinting – this was the evil of the world before him, and yet surely there was kindness in those eyes. "You see two pieces of magic before you, theirs and mine. The bindings cannot be cut, the stake cannot be removed – that was their doing. But no sword can harm me, no blade can remove my head – that is my magic. You see below me

275

the swords of those who tried, and their fate was only to nourish me further."

Will looked at the pile of ancient swords on the floor beneath Labraid's head. He'd imagined them as some sort of taunt, but counting them now, he saw how determined these people had been to kill the Suspended King.

"Then what am I to do?"

"All this was prophesied," said Labraid. "I said no one can remove my head, but in truth, no one but the one can remove it, and that one is you, William of Mercia."

Will turned and looked at Eloise, confused now, asking her with his expression if it had all been for this, that he might be Lorcan Labraid's executioner. Eloise shook her head, making clear she was no closer to understanding.

Will turned back to Labraid and said, "My Lord, I have not travelled through seven centuries merely to end your life. There must be some way to free you from these bindings."

"A true prince among men, but you of all people should know that one king dies and another takes his place. My reign is at an end, and I gladly relinquish it to you, unfettered, to achieve the power that has long been yours, and fulfil the words of the prophecy." Labraid could see Will's continuing reluctance and said, "I am a part of you already, just as the other kings are a part

276

of you, but when I die, if it is at your hand, all of my power will become yours. Only then will your destiny be fulfilled."

"And Eloise?"

Labraid's eyes flicked across to her and he smiled. "Every king needs a queen. My power will become your power, the power to sire children, to reinvigorate the line, but above all, the power to make any like us, even Eloise. It matters not if she carries the line, for the line begins again with you."

Will did not need to turn to know how Eloise would have responded to that. Yet Will's heart was suddenly heavy, with sadness and disappointment and, yes, betrayal, because he knew instinctively that Labraid was lying.

Keeping his tone even, he said, "Did I choose well?"

"I believe the choice was made for you." There it was, Will was certain of it, a hint of regret in Labraid's voice. Whatever Eloise's part in this, it was not to become a queen of the underworld, to reign alongside Will. That role had been for Imogen alone, and Will suspected Labraid bitterly regretted that it was Eloise standing here with them.

"Why did Elfleda try to kill her?"

"Poor Elfleda. She was driven by jealousy, and by misunderstanding. She thought I would rise again, that

277

Eloise would be my queen, replacing her."

Will was about to speak, but the world briefly seemed to shift about them, a wrenching noise somewhere deep in the earth. The chamber shimmered, looking momentarily less solid around them. From the tunnels far beyond Will could hear the restless and uneasy movement of leathery wings.

"What was that?"

Labraid said, "Time is short. Make haste, or what has been opened will close again and our opportunity will be lost. You must act now."

Will took a step back, so shocked was he to hear Labraid using the same words as the witches. Had they been Labraid's creation? They had talked of serving another, and yet, no, he thought back on their actions and knew that it couldn't be so, that the witches had served Eloise. Perhaps they alone had sought to protect her and keep her safe.

The earth trembled again, the walls becoming fluid once more.

Eloise sounded nervous as she said, "Will, I don't think we have much time."

"William of Mercia, if you do not strike now we are both doomed to our current fates for eternity. Strike!"

His voice boomed. The chamber had not returned to normal, but seemed to be shaking and distorting around them, and yet Will needed more time. He knew, at some level he simply knew, that this was wrong, that Eloise had no place in what was being offered him. And if Eloise had no place in it, then Will did not want the power he was being offered, no matter how great. She was a part of this, she had to be.

His mind raced, over the paintings on the walls in the storeroom, over the words of the witches on the many occasions he had seen them, the words of Harriet's spirit, "I am not here, sir." He thought of Rachel looking at her burned tarot book, the pages showing the Hanged Man adjacent to Death, but death was not always death, Rachel had said. He thought of his mother, clutching the pendant around her neck as she'd descended back into the spirit world.

His thoughts were moving so quickly, they were as distorted as the room about him.

"Will?"

And there it was, a voice, his name, complete clarity. There was so little time, but he understood at last. He understood!

Eloise. He had chosen Eloise, and Eloise was death.

He approached her now and held her by the shoulders, looking into her eyes, urgent.

"Eloise, you need to listen to me. In a moment I will sever his head. Something will happen, something will begin to happen to me as soon as I do that, and you must be ready. He's lying about your place in this. You have only one role here. As soon as I have done my part, you must take the sword from my hand." She started to shake her head, terrified. Even this fitted, he saw it now. The one thing she had resisted all along was taking up a sword because at some level, subconsciously, she had surely known the role she would have to play. "You take the sword from my hand and with all your might, you strike me on the neck and remove my head. You have seen it done. You know how. Do it quickly."

She was crying as she said, "You know I won't do that!"

Labraid called out, "William of Mercia, the time . . ."

"You must, Eloise. Do you love me?" She was too upset even to answer. "Then you must do this. I wish I could explain, but we have no time, not now. If you love me, you will do it."

He kissed her, felt the warmth and the softness of her lips against his, and at last he felt no pain. He pulled away again, wiped the tears from her face. "Eloise, I have waited over seven hundred years for you, and it was worth every minute."

Labraid's voice boomed over the chaos, "William of . . ."

Will pushed away from Eloise and swung hard,

the sword slicing into the Suspended King's neck before Labraid exploded in a mass of blue light which disappeared instantly. For a moment there was an after-image of Labraid, as if drawn in vapour, but then the mist flew towards Will, clinging to him, becoming part of him.

He could feel its impact immediately, something happening within the fibres of his being. He threw the sword on to the floor in front of Eloise. He fell to his knees, pulling his collar apart as noble Edgar had done.

"Now, Eloise, or it will be too late."

"I can't," she said, shaking her head, but she picked up the sword. He knew she could do this, knew she was strong enough.

The room was still trembling, his own flesh felt as if it was exploding with the new powers he had gained. From the tunnels, he could hear the shrieks of all those devils so desperate to serve him. And evil – evil was already within him, taking root.

"Now!"

It seemed eternal, the moment between his cry and her reluctant positioning of the sword. And then she looked into his eyes and appeared to find the strength and the resolve he knew she possessed. She raised the sword, and as tears streamed down her cheeks, she brought it down swiftly towards his neck.

Darkness, instant. He heard someone call his name and thought it was Eloise, filling him with a terrible sadness. But it wasn't her, and it was more than one person, and he realised now that it was his family, calling him home at last, a death he'd been travelling towards for more than seven centuries. Dimly, a light appeared in the distance, and he fell happily through the darkness towards it.

31

She heard a voice. For a moment she thought it was Will, then realised it wasn't, a realisation that filled her with a terrible sadness. Her eyes opened and she saw the chamber around her, bright and clean.

It took a moment for her to understand that she was lying on the floor. She sat up and saw that there were lights positioned around the walls. Yet it was undoubtedly the same chamber, one where it seemed just a few moments before, Will had killed Lorcan Labraid, and Eloise had killed Will.

She could still hear the voice, coming from along one of the other tunnels, not the passage she and Will had used to enter the chamber. But the tunnels were also bright, and she could tell from the tone and rhythm of the voice that this was a tour guide.

To herself, Eloise said aloud, "No, I did not dream this!"

"No, you did not."

She jumped to her feet, turning. Across the chamber,

seven familiar figures stood with their heads bowed, the hoods of their robes concealing their faces. Eloise almost laughed with relief to see them there. She had not dreamt or imagined this, she was not losing her mind – or at least, if she was, it was still happily lost.

"What . . .? I don't understand, what happened?"

The one who spoke stepped forward, her head still bowed, as she said, "On the floor behind you, there is your answer."

Eloise turned, searching the floor, unable to see anything, and the voice of the tour guide was getting closer. Then she saw it, almost at her feet. She bent down and picked it up, the pendant that had hung around Will's neck, one half of the boar's head relief, the letter "W" on the back. The leather strap had been sliced, with a sword wielded by her.

The spirit's voice was immediately behind her now as it said softly, "The circle is broken and is made whole again."

Eloise turned and cried out in shock. The spirit had raised her head, but the melted features Eloise had become so used to were gone, and in their place was only the kindly face of a middle-aged lady, her eyes a dazzling blue. She smiled, but it was if she was unaware that she appeared any different.

Eloise tried to think of what she wanted to say, but

there were so many things that none would come, and in the end she said only, "Is everything undone? This chamber, the . . ."

"Death cannot be undone." The spirit took a step backwards and bowed a little. "Death cannot be undone." She turned and joined the other six, and with sparks and jolts of light playing across their robes, they walked through the chamber walls and disappeared.

"Then, in the late nineteenth century . . ." The voice was deafening now and Eloise walked towards it quickly, just as the guide stepped into the chamber with a curious and eager group of Japanese tourists pressing behind him. He saw Eloise and said, "Oh, I do beg your pardon."

The man, wearing a beige jacket with a flowery tie, stepped into the chamber and to one side, and the Japanese tourists poured in afterwards.

"So sorry," said the man. "Once they're all in you can make your escape."

"Thank you," said Eloise, and blinked as one of the tourists took her picture, the flash briefly dazzling, reminding her inevitably of Will.

She walked into the passage as if in a dream, the sound of the guided tour continuing behind her. Was this the world Wyndham had so feared? And without knowing where she was going, she followed what felt like the right path.

As she walked, she took the other pendant and retied the leather, putting it over her head. Then quite suddenly she saw the outside world ahead and emerged into a beautiful sunlit day, a blue sky. How many hours had she been unconscious, she wondered. And yet, what were hours, when the world had somehow been reordered about her?

She'd emerged on to a well-manicured gravel path on the side of a small hill and was just trying to get her bearings when she noticed the familiar roofline of the school down below. She started to walk towards it across the parkland and then stopped as she saw someone coming in the opposite direction.

Curiosity turned to shock and anxiety as she realised it was Miss Lawrence. Even after everything Eloise had been through, she felt her heart racing and didn't know what she would say, how she could begin to answer the questions the teacher would now have for her.

Miss Lawrence saw her and waved, and came towards her in big strides. She was some distance away when she said, "Ah, Eloise, you'll be perfect."

"I'm sorry?"

Miss Lawrence didn't answer, but waited until she'd reached her, the teacher's expression showing no signs of what Eloise believed had happened to her last night.

"You couldn't do me a huge favour, could you?"

She shook her head as if trying to express quite how insane things were right now. "The whole place is in pandemonium this afternoon and Mr Asquith's frazzled, frankly, what with Dr Higson just disappearing."

"He's disappeared?"

"Didn't you know?" She clearly relished the prospect of sharing the news. "He went off to visit Alex Shawcross's parents. Poor Alex, if only we'd realised he was so unhappy."

Death cannot be undone, thought Eloise – it made sense now, and she knew before Miss Lawrence continued that Higson would never be found.

"Anyway, he must have come back because his car's here, but he's disappeared off the face of the earth."

"Oh, how strange. And nothing unusual to suggest . . ."

"Nothing at all. Just vanished. Miss Bettencourt thinks he blamed himself for Alex, but who can tell?"

Eloise nodded, but was sorry in a way that Miss Lawrence knew nothing of what had happened the night before. Then, with a feeling of dislocation, she realised that for Miss Lawrence nothing *had* happened the night before. It was as if time had split in two, and Eloise alone had been on the other side of it.

"What was the favour, Miss Lawrence?"

"Yes, of course, slightly jollier matters – the new boy.

Would you be a darling and go over to the new house, get William Dangrave, bring him to the school, show him round, help him settle in. He won't be boarding of course, but . . ."

"William Dangrave?" Her voice sounded outside her own body, as if someone else had spoken the name for her.

Miss Lawrence looked at Eloise as if she was being wilfully obtuse, and said, "I've only been talking about his arrival since the beginning of term. Sophia Hamilton was going to chaperone him, but of course she banged her head yesterday." She raised her eyes skywards as if describing an episode of silliness. "But you're probably a better fit anyway. I think you share some of the same interests so you'll even be in the same classes." She looked at her watch, and said, "Oh Lord, I really must fly. Just be nice, and don't mention Dr Higson." She started to walk away, but turned back briefly. "Or Alex."

And she was gone. Eloise had walked out of the burial chamber as if in a dream, but it was nothing compared with the daze with which she walked towards the new house. She realised too that her heart was beating dangerously fast now.

She was shaken out of it only as she reached the house and a man came out carrying tins of paint.

"Excuse me, do you know where I might find William Dangrave."

The man shrugged, but then said, "Oh, I do know, over at the abbey ruins."

"Thank you."

"You're welcome."

She walked along the side of the house to the ruins and there saw three people. A middle-aged man and woman, and a boy of about her own age. They were all blond and though the parents were tanned, the boy looked incredibly pale. They were looking around the ruins with some interest.

Eloise approached and when she was still a little way off, she said, "William Dangrave?"

The boy turned and smiled at her, somewhat blankly, followed by his parents.

"I'm William Dangrave."

The voice had come from off to Eloise's right. She turned and stared and felt briefly unsteady. Beyond a low wall, in one of the neighbouring ruined rooms, Will was standing looking at her. Will. He was wearing casual clothes, his skin was a little tanned, but otherwise he looked exactly the same.

She smiled, let out a single laugh and said, "Hello."

"Hi."

She walked towards him, stepping over the wall,

feeling weightless as she landed on the grass. She threw her arms round him without another thought and held on to him, feeling the warmth of his body against hers, breathing in the scent of him.

Then she heard him speak, felt him speak, the vibrations through his ribcage. And a heart, she felt a heart beating inside him.

"Now *that's* the kind of welcome I was hoping for. Hello."

Eloise stepped back and looked at him in wonder. "Sorry, I . . . you're Australian."

He laughed and said, "That's . . . kind of what happens when you're brought up in Australia. Er, and you are?"

"I'm Eloise. I was sent to show you around the school."

He looked at her, puzzled now, as if she'd broken a dream, and said, "Eloise. What a beautiful name. It suits you."

"Thank you. And you're William Dangrave."

"Will actually, but yeah. Dad's a history buff so I was named after William the Wise from the thirteenth century."

"Were you?" Eloise laughed, full of joy, full of hope and pride and every good emotion, full of love for someone who'd been dead for hundreds of years, thanks to her.

"What's funny?"

"Nothing, I'm just . . . happy. Ignore me." She looked at the house, making countless calculations, noting among other things that they had never become Heston-Dangraves, that the titles had surely survived. She looked at him again, and said, "So you're going to be the Earl of Mercia one day."

He pulled a face, acknowledging how alarming it was, and said, "No, I'm the Earl of Mercia now. You know, once my dad succeeded to the Dukedom . . ."

"It's a Dukedom now?"

He looked at her askance, suspecting perhaps that she was making fun of him, and said, "Only for the last four hundred years – I can see how you might have missed that."

"I'm not as flaky as I seem. Come on, let's go to the school." He looked reluctant at the mention of school, but walked with her, out of the ruins and across the park. "It's a great school actually, you'll love it."

"Well, I'm liking the idea a bit more since I met you." He walked for a few paces and said, "Actually, when you told me your name . . . no. Look, I swear to God this isn't a chat-up line, but I do feel like I've met you before somewhere."

"Not a chat-up line? Why, don't you think I'm attractive?"

"I didn't mean that . . . no, you're really . . . I mean . . ." She laughed, and he realised she was teasing. He laughed too and playfully poked her on the arm.

As she walked, she lifted her hand and felt the two pendants hanging around her neck, and she knew that one day she would give one of them to this boy walking beside her. Yet still she could not help but feel a little sadness for the boy she had lost, to his own time, where for all his wisdom he could never have foreseen that she would one day walk here with his namesake and double, the sun warm on their skin.

Eloise turned and looked at him. "It must have been an upheaval, leaving at your age, coming here."

"You're not winding me up now?" He was smiling, but she shook her head. "Yeah, I didn't wanna come. I mean, I'm glad I did now, well, I think I might be . . . oh, shut up, Will. Simple fact is, I didn't wanna come, but you know, when you're sixteen, you go where your parents go."

"So, you could go back in a couple of years if you want to."

"True, but who knows, in a couple of years I might not want to."

She looked at him, smiled, then laughed at the thought, and said, "That's the main thing, isn't it? You'll have a choice. We won't be sixteen forever."

"Also true. Could you imagine anything worse?"

They both laughed then, and walked on down the gentle grassy slope, with the old house basking in the sunlight below them.

32

The circle is broken and is made whole again.

There they walk, Will and Eloise, leaving the ancient ruins behind, setting off across the parkland in the sunshine on a warm spring afternoon. Eloise will give him one of those pendants some day soon, and he'll treasure it. And though they're young, they will stay together and eventually marry.

In that, Eloise's distant ancestor will see the fruition of the final curse she uttered from her pyre as the flames rose around her, that her descendants would take this Earldom unto themselves. It was always meant to be.

What Eloise will never do is try to tell Will of the things she experienced in the months before they met. For she understands that in his world, in the world she now inhabits herself, those things never happened.

At least, some of those things never happened. Time and space may overlap, but it is as the witch said, not everything can be undone around the ragged edges of that overlap. Death cannot be undone. The girl knows that too, though she cares little for it now as she walks with this boy.

Dr Higson will never be found. Alex Shawcross committed suicide, a fact which cannot be changed. All that matters to the girl now is that goodness triumphed, that the Will she knew and the Will she has just met represent that goodness.

But it is time for me to take my leave of them, as they walk towards their school and their future together. I am death, and my part in their tale is done. To walk in the sun, to love, these things are not for me now. I have a part to play in my own prophecy.

So my eye takes flight across the landscape, leaving them behind, over the new house, over the city on this beautiful day that cannot be mine. I stop briefly to look down on the café in one of the old narrow streets, The Whole Earth, closed this afternoon as a woman comes to terms with the mysterious road accident that killed her husband.

I do not linger, but move on, beyond the city walls, out towards the large municipal cemetery. There I see another woman, tending the grave of her fifteen-year-old son, weeping quietly, sensing in some way that she always knew this day would come. Is it not obvious, looking down on this sad scene, that she feels the failure is hers, that she brought the boy up wrong, that she should never have allowed Mr Wyndham to take him.

Oh, I wish more than anything, I wish so desperately, that I could reach out and touch that grieving mother's shoulder, assure her with my presence that her tears are in vain. I wish I could tell her that her son is not dead but merely at rest, and that even if she were to dig in that spot at the end of her long life, she would find his body untouched by time or worms.

For that is the least of what I know. I am not dead – I am become death. My name is Marcus Jenkins. I was fifteen years old when I was struck down. And for all the passing of the years, I will still be fifteen in my person when you who read this are old, then dead, then forgotten.

Acknowledgements

As ever, I owe a great deal to my agent, Sarah Molloy, and all at AM Heath. Thanks also to my editor, Stella Paskins, for expertly guiding me to the end of . . . *Death*. And thanks to Elizabeth Law, and all at Egmont in the UK and USA. Jane Tait has shown a masterful attention to detail as my copy editor, and Sharon Chai has produced stunning designs for the books, so I owe my gratitude to both of them. Finally, I have to mention you, the reader. Writing this trilogy has been immensely rewarding, and a big part of that has been thanks to the many people who've written, and continue to write, to tell me how much they've enjoyed the books – it matters more than you could know, because a book is an ephemeral thing which is never real until it's read.

> *"...we are such stuff as dreams are made on;*
> *and our little life is rounded with a sleep..."*

ELECTRIC MONKEY

To find out more about other fantastic books
for young adult readers check out the brilliant new
ELECTRIC MONKEY website:

Trailers

Blogs

News and Reviews

Competitions

Downloads

Free stuff

Author interviews

 Like us on Facebook

Follow us on Twitter